Family Spirit

Diane McKinney-Whetstone

AMISTAD
An Imprint of HarperCollinsPublishers

Family Spirit

a novel

Without limiting the exclusive rights of any author, contributor or the publisher of this publication, any unauthorized use of this publication to train generative artificial intelligence (AI) technologies is expressly prohibited. HarperCollins also exercise their rights under Article 4(3) of the Digital Single Market Directive 2019/790 and expressly reserve this publication from the text and data mining exception.

FAMILY SPIRIT. Copyright © 2025 by Diane McKinney-Whetstone. All rights reserved. Printed in the United States of America. No part of this book may be used or reproduced in any manner whatsoever without written permission except in the case of brief quotations embodied in critical articles and reviews. For information, address HarperCollins Publishers, 195 Broadway, New York, NY 10007. In Europe, HarperCollins Publishers, Macken House, 39/40 Mayor Street Upper, Dublin 1, D01 C9W8, Ireland.

HarperCollins books may be purchased for educational, business, or sales promotional use. For information, please email the Special Markets Department at SPsales@harpercollins.com.

harpercollins.com

FIRST EDITION

Designed by Yvonne Chan
Art on pages iii, 7, 71, 193 © Getty Images; © Shutterstock
Chapter opener art © 百合 須藤/stock.adobe.com

Library of Congress Cataloging-in-Publication Data:

Names: McKinney-Whetstone, Diane, author.
Title: Family spirit / Diane McKinney-Whetstone.
Description: First edition. | New York, NY: Amistad, 2025.
Identifiers: LCCN 2025009146 (print) | LCCN 2025009147 (ebook) |
ISBN 9780063395428 (hardcover) | ISBN 9780063395442 (epub)
Subjects: LCGFT: Paranormal fiction. | Novels.
Classification: LCC PS3563.C3825 F36 2025 (print) | LCC PS3563.C3825 (ebook) |
DDC 813/.54--dc23/eng/20250227
LC record available at https://lccn.loc.gov/2025009146
LC ebook record available at https://lccn.loc.gov/2025009147

25 26 27 28 29 LBC 5 4 3 2 1

For Lula

For still the vision awaits its appointed time;
it hastens to the end—it will not lie.

Habakkuk 2:3

A False Start

June 2019, Nona's Writing Room, Philadelphia Exurbs

Nona hunched over her laptop, moving her fingers frenetically like Thelonious Monk getting down on a Steinway; senses engaged, stomach whirling, pings firing in her brain, leaving a euphoric coating. She was early in the writing of a novel centered on a West Philly family, a clairvoyant family, circa, well, she wasn't sure yet about the time period, she was unsure about much of the story, just trusted that everything she needed to understand about that world would rise up from the detail like a dream with nonsensical veers that she could step into and reconfigure.

So she took time with the detail as she looked out the window in the room where she wrote, which faced a sun-swathed meadow. She was miles away from the urban scape of West Philly's Fifty-Second, which she imagined now, where the air smelled of popcorn and new patent leather, and where cool cats with amplified swagger stopped mid-stroll in front of the Nixon Theater to strike a redheaded matchstick against the sole of their new Florsheims, then touched the flame to the cigarette that hung from the corner of their mouth like a jazz note dangling. Ribbons of music streamed from the Club Aqua Lounge, enticing big-legged women in cinnamon-colored hose and wide-shouldered men in suits and shades to come in and sip from short glasses filled with gold liquid, maybe sneak in a slow drag under the press of low lights and the high-fidelity sounds of Sam Cooke crooning "Bring It On Home to Me."

Yeah, this is good, she thought, aware now that the time period would be the early '60s. But then she heard that voice in her head saying, "Same ol', same ol'."

"So what, nothing's new anyhow," she talked back to the voice, refusing to allow it to disrupt her groove. Right now, as she crafted this Aqua Lounge scene, she could practically inhale the smoke swirling from the Kool filter tips; could taste the crisply fried butterfish, the burnt-edged candied yams on platters floated by waitresses who called everyone "baby" or "sweet thing."

A blue-bulbed chandelier spilled a moody vibe over the square of dance floor. A couple bopped to "Baby I Need Your Loving." Their moves were intricate and smooth, and people hooted and called out, "Y'all go 'head with your bad selves and don't hurt nothing," and "When I'mma see y'all on *Ed Sullivan*." Nona smiled herself as she described the dancing woman laughing with an open mouth, seeming at first to be having a good time. Her eyes didn't crinkle with the laugh, though, and Nona wondered if the mismatch meant that she was sad. She was wearing a Diana Ross–type bouffant wig, a reddish brown that picked up the colors in her paisley blouse. The blouse, unbuttoned to her cleavage, hung too loosely. When her dance partner twirled her around, there was a barely visible imprint of a safety pin under her blouse at the top of her red skirt. Had she merely lost a button with no time to replace it, or had she lost a lot of weight and the pin was holding her skirt up? It was weight loss, Nona decided, unexplained dramatic loss of weight indicative of a serious illness. That was why her laughter hadn't reached her eyes. That's why she was dancing so hard right now, trying to dance away the advancing mortality moving through her bones.

Damn, and she's so young, Nona thought as she swiveled her desk chair away from the window with its view of the meadow filled with wildflowers and promise.

Her chest tightened at the prospect of allowing the dancing woman further onto the page. She'd been doing this long enough to know that dissecting her characters to render their mess of desires and foibles and conditions meant also having to peer deep into her own self. And she had her own condition: a cyst on her pancreas. Her doctor had ordered an MRI, "just to rule things out," she'd told Nona. Nona had put off the MRI, and this morning there was a message in her MyChart portal reminding her that the imaging needed to be scheduled.

She turned back to her laptop and selected the section with the dancing woman. She hit delete. She was glad she hadn't given her a name yet. She tried to push on through the scene without her. But she was still there, hauntingly, still dancing, her blouse and skirt growing looser until her clothes were on the floor. Nona gasped at the image of her still bopping, her bones twirling like those Halloween skeletons that had horrified her as a child. The whole of the Aqua Lounge was oblivious, though, save the blue-bulbed chandelier that suddenly went dark, out of respect.

She hit select all as she closed her ears to the detail and characters clamoring to stay. "Nope, nope, nope, not going there," she said. Then she deleted the thing.

The explosion of the blank page offended her eyes. She pressed them shut to moisten them, then blinked harder and harder until her eyes teared. She wiped her face, blew her nose, thought she needed to take some time off from the writing. She couldn't take time off, though. She had a book deadline, bills to pay, and a pilot husband who would return soon from a weeklong rotation, scattering her writing focus like breadcrumbs that led nowhere.

She made another pot of coffee, chewed a pack of sugarless gum, stared down the blank screen until something happened. A new setting happened. A suburban shopping center under a smiling sun.

"Shopping mall? Really?" The voice again. "Could you possibly find a more mundane setting?"

"Leave me alone," she said to the voice. She was back in the flow as she depicted the little girl she'd originally imagined for the story: wide-eyed with pinchable cheeks, freshly braided hair, diamond posts in her pierced ears, and a yellow denim jacket that matched her sneakers and My Little Pony purse. Nona named the child Ayana. Ayana would be a keeper, filled as she was with innocence, possibilities, and, especially, powers.

Nona's breathing slowed to near normal as she settled

down, as she allowed herself to sift into the new setting of the discombobulated dream of this story's unfolding. She felt safely distanced from Fifty-Second Street and the back-in-the-day Aqua Lounge inhabited by the nameless woman in the brown and red blouse. Girl could really dance, though, and already Nona missed her.

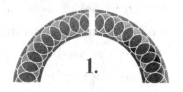

1.
Shopping

It was seventy degrees, ocean-blue sky, the sun like a mound of lemon drops convening, no glare. The air was as sweet as Nat King Cole's voice flowing from the brand-new 2004 MINI Cooper as the car turned into the shopping center. The car's driver loved Nat's rendition of "Unforgettable," so he'd tuned his CD player to automatic repeat, mainly to distract himself from the pain in his heart. This was not the typical my-woman-did-me-wrong pain but real center-of-chest pain that had prompted him to go to the urgent care next to Marshalls. By the time he had the facility in his sights, the pain in his chest had grown so crushing that he could no longer steer, brake, mash his horn, call out "Lord help me." Cruelly, though, he could see; he could hear. He saw the glass front of Marshalls speeding toward him. He heard Nat King Cole's lovely crooning overtaken by screams pitched so high, he thought the screams, not his MINI Cooper, had caused the storefront to burst and shatter.

"Ayana," one woman shrieked over and over, "Ayana, my God, Ayana." In his delirium, he had the thought that as soon as he was able to stop the car, he'd help the woman find Ayana. But he was already stopped by the tangle of shopping carts and a mammoth stuffed Easter Bunny with folded arms hugging bags of jelly beans and pink and purple boxes filled with chocolate-covered coconut eggs.

Six-year-old Ayana was skipping next to Lorna, her mother, as they entered Marshalls. She pulled her hand from her mother's and smiled and waved to a woman sitting out front on a mobility scooter. The woman reminded her of GG, her great-grandmother, with her oak-colored skin and white cottony hair styled in a puffy upsweep.

"Aren't you a cutie-pie, and I love those beads on your braids," the woman said.

Ayana said thank you and asked the woman if she could tell her a secret and then whispered in her ear. The woman giggled and whispered in Ayana's ear, and they went back and forth like that until the woman announced she'd better scoot over to Michaels to meet her daughter. After Ayana watched the woman get beyond the glass front of Marshalls, she ran into the store to the sound of her mother's exasperated voice.

"What were you doing? I thought you were right next to me, and who was that lady, and what were you all whispering about?"

"About the car."

Family Spirit

"Car?" Lorna asked as she pulled Ayana across the store toward the designer section, breathing through her mouth as she began rifling through the jumbled racks in this Marshalls. She was trying to avoid the smells of polyester, plastic, and tin, the smells of imitation, leftovers, last year's unwanted. She especially hated being in here the day before Easter, when everything was already picked over, but she was still trying to satisfy the insatiable childhood wanting that bouts of psychotherapy had failed to cure: that she might feel new on Easter Sunday morning.

She swiped hangers across poles and kept one eye on Ayana skipping around a display of artificial peace lilies. Rusted memories from her own childhood surged, and she saw herself and her sisters marching in a row behind their mother, going to Easter service in itchy donated garb. Only their hair was new, freshly washed, softly pressed into upswept ringlets, such pretty girls, people said, such a shame they'd lost their father that way. Her sisters followed their mother's lead as they strutted into church, owning the attitude that they were good enough as they were. That attitude was lost on Lorna. She imagined people felt sorry for them with their poor selves.

"We're not poor," her mother would insist. "Poor people don't have what they need. We have everything we need. We're just a little temporarily broke is all. Broke but not broken."

Was there a difference? Lorna wondered back then. Wondered it now as she peered at the price tag on a mint-colored linen suit, which was at least more affordable than the one she'd just returned to Neiman Marcus because she could no longer justify the full-price expense. She was a local model who hadn't had a booking in over a month. And she'd just learned earlier today that her husband, Miles, would have to settle for the kill fee for a *Black Enterprise* piece he'd worked on for a dozen weeks.

She looked around for Ayana, who had moved from the plastic lilies to a shelf of mannequin heads sporting paisley scarves. "Please stay where I can see you," she called out to Ayana. "Why don't you go play with that huge Easter bunny in the window, isn't it cute?" Lorna coaxed.

"I can't," Ayana said, pouting.

"Why not," Lorna asked, talking more to the suit than to Ayana.

"Because it's too close to the car crash—"

"Car crash?" Lorna asked.

"Yeah, the red car in the window—"

"Red car in the window? I don't see any red car," Lorna said, glancing toward the window. "What are you talking about?" She held the suit skirt to her waist to test the length.

"Nothing," Ayana said, swallowing the rest of it and shaking her head so the beads on her braided bangs bounced against her forehead.

She moved farther away from her mother and told her she was going to hide. "You have to come find me," she said, and then disappeared behind a display of skinny jeans.

"No, ma'am, we are not playing hide-and-seek in this store," Lorna warned as she said excuse me over and over and maneuvered past people to snatch up a yellow raw silk blouse on a hanger marked extra-small. The blouse was extra-large, though, and Lorna cursed under her breath and looked around for Ayana. She didn't see her. She called her name in the voice that came from deep in her throat, that meant Ayana was in trouble. But at least as Lorna tried to find her, she was drawn away from the storefront that exploded right then as the red MINI Cooper came barreling on in through the Marshalls window as if it, too, were short on cash and looking to find an Easter outfit on the cheap.

For a nanosecond after, the collective horror of a car crashing into the store was sucked up like a grand inhalation, and the world inside Marshalls went silent and still. Then the exhale tilted the store with screams and shouts and foot stomps running away from the car, toward it, around it, as if everyone in here were involved in a frenetic line dance with no DJ to call out the next steps. Lorna's voice ranged from screeching to guttural as she cried out Ayana's name. She clutched the linen suit to her chest as if the suit would save them. The irony was not lost on her that had it not been for the suit, for her conceit, her obsession with a new Easter outfit, she wouldn't be here. She'd be home helping Miles work through his deflation over the rejected article that contained pieces of his soul. *Your claiming-to-be-clairvoyant family shoulda warned you not to quit your day job instead of encouraging you to live your dream. Some dream,* she'd thought but not verbalized when he'd told her his piece had been rejected. Though she sensed that she may as well have used her words anyhow, the way his face had collapsed as he waited for her to say something. What would his face do when she told him that because of her, they'd lost their only child. "Father have mercy," she said as she pushed toward the wreck. She saw the oversize bunny first, the poor bunny with its foam insides protruding, mashed chocolate eggs and jelly beans scattered like a damaged memorial for a child killed. Somebody was opening the car door, somebody else down on the floor looking to see if a person was trapped under the car. She wailed out Ayana's name as she took in the smells of fumes and gasoline and burnt rubber. She almost slipped on twisted metal, shards of glass, wondered if her daughter's diamond earrings were among the thousands of gleaming specks carpeting the floor. She prayed she wouldn't see Ayana's My Little Pony purse, her bright yellow jacket, even as she saw Ayana's life flash in front of her: the golden-brown baby with the tousled crown of thick curly hair who laughed out loud at a week old, who spoke in full sentences at a year, who had a wide gushy smile like her dad's and a warm, friendly demeanor like his, too, unlike her own; she could be cold. "Why pretty women so mean," Miles would tease her when he was trying to bring her out of a mood. Was this her punishment for her meanness? "Lord no, please no," she called out as she spun around in circles. Then she saw the pink beads that adorned Ayana's braided bangs, followed by the whole of her child running and jumping and waving her hands in the air. "Ah, ah, ah" was all she gasped as she scooped Ayana into her arms and covered her with the suit and ran with her to the back of the store through a dusty corridor marked "Employees Only." She needed to protect Ayana, shaken Ayana, and herself from what she imagined was the mangled driver, the possibility even that the car might catch fire, might explode. She could already hear sirens as they exited Marshalls through the loading dock. She slowed herself as they walked through the parking lot and approached her car. She put Ayana down. "It's okay, we're okay, right? You're okay, right?" Ayana nodded even as she stood there shivering. Lorna draped the mint-colored linen jacket around Ayana and put her in the back seat and then climbed in next to her. She smoothed her fingers down Ayana's face and told her to breathe. "Real slow, real deep, just breathe with Mommy, in and out, in and out."

Ayana did, then she put her head on her mother's chest, and they snuggled like that as Lorna watched the fire trucks and emergency vehicles crowding around Marshalls.

✦ ✦ ✦

Later that night as Lorna tucked Ayana's braids under the satin sleep cap, she allowed her hand to linger on Ayana's forehead.

"I'm not sick," Ayana announced, assuming from her mother's wide-with-worry eyes that she was checking for a fever.

"I know you're not. I just want to make sure you're all right after that accident at Marshalls."

"I'm okay, and everybody else is, too, right?"

"That's right, they said on the news that it was a miracle no one was hurt other than the man who lost control of his car."

Ayana nodded. "I know."

"How'd you know?"

"I heard you telling Aunt Sis."

Ayana studied her mother's face, glad that it was clear of makeup. She thought Lorna was prettier without makeup. Ayana could tell that her father thought so, too, because just now when he came to kiss Ayana good night and her mother said she wanted to talk to Ayana a little longer, he looked at her mother's unpainted face and broke out into a smile shaped like a perfect crescent moon.

"Are you okay, Mommy?" Ayana asked as her eyes took in the line between her mother's eyebrows. She was glad Lorna wasn't looking in the mirror this instant or she'd be cursing at the wrinkle.

"Mommy's okay," Lorna said on a sigh. "But I have to ask you, remember when I suggested you play with the stuffed bunny, you said you couldn't because of the red car, and then a few minutes later, the car drove into the store, did the lady you were talking to say something about the car?"

"Noooo. I said something to her."

"What did you say to her?" Lorna took her voice down to a whisper.

"The car was gonna crash." Ayana matched her mother's breathy tone.

"But how did you know?"

"I just knew."

"Did you dream it?"

Ayana shook her head vigorously.

"Well, did you see it somehow when you were wide awake?"

"You mean when you were giving back your suit?"

"Yes, when we still at Neiman's, did you see it then?"

"No." Ayana shook her head slowly this time, wondering if she'd done something wrong.

"Well, how did you know about the accident?"

"I just knew?" Ayana asked more than answered.

Lorna rose, and her eyes looked beyond the stuffed animals crammed along the top of Ayana's bookshelf. Ayana feared that her mother was going to retreat to that unreachable place the way she'd done weeks before, when Lorna's mother had died and Lorna would sit on the ottoman in front of the window, her back so straight and still as she stared outside, not even turning around when Ayana pretended to cry to get her attention. She forced a laugh now to pull her mother back before she lost her again. "I was just being silly, Mommy. I didn't know anything about that car crashing."

"Are you fibbing to me?"

"No, I'm not," she said, crying now.

"Well, then why are you crying?"

"I don't know, I feel bad, because—because— What did I do that was wrong?"

Lorna sighed with her whole body so that even her shoulders slumped; her shoulders rarely slumped. She sat on the bed and pulled Ayana in a hug. "You didn't do anything wrong. Mommy just wants you to understand that there is no way for you to know that things will happen before they happen."

"You mean like Daddy's crazy-ass family?"

Lorna pulled Ayana closer, and Ayana could hear the smile in her voice. "I see I have to start censoring myself when your little ears are around. Don't you tell your daddy you overheard me saying that. But they are weird. And you are not like them."

"But my last name is Mace, like their last name is Mace—"

"Well, they're your daddy's people—"

"And you said I look pretty like them."

"Absolutely you do. You have their big eyes and high cheekbones." Lorna smoothed her fingers over Ayana's brows. "And you're smart like some of them, too, like your daddy and your daddy's sister, your aunt Lil—"

"Aunt Lil who we can't talk about in front of GG?"

"Yes, we definitely don't mention Aunt Lil around her."

"Why?"

"Because she's upset with your aunt Lil."

"Are you upset with GG because she's upset with Aunt Lil?"

"What makes you ask that?"

"You never come with me and Daddy when we go over there."

"I don't visit there often—"

"Never," Ayana interrupted.

"Okay, never," Lorna said as she sat all the way up. The smile in her voice had reversed direction and moved into the vocal register that produced a clang so sharp that Ayana angled herself to get a better view of her mother's face. The line was on her forehead again, deeper than ever.

"Here's the thing: I keep my distance from them because they believe they can see into the future. And I don't believe in that, and I don't want you to, either, because I'm afraid I'll lose you to their beliefs."

Ayana thought her mother was about to cry, the way her eyes got big and soupy. That made Ayana cry again, and she put her arms around her mother's neck and said, "You won't ever lose me, Mommy, I promise you forever." She pushed her head into her mother's chest and listened to her heart thumps and tried to swallow away the feeling caught in her throat that her mother was wrong, because she was exactly like her daddy's people.

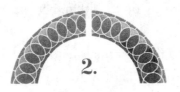

2.

Guilt

2019

Ayana so internalized her mother's warnings about being lost to her if she was like them that she hid the alikeness. Lied to her mother about participating in their rituals; lied to the Maces when they asked her if she'd yet to feel the Knowing—their name for their inherited clairvoyance that they traced back to the late 1700s. She kept the guilt over her lies mostly contained in tiny pellets in the pit of her stomach. Though sometimes they'd pop, sending hurtful burns all the way to her throat, and she'd taste ash, like now, as she was about to lie to her new guy while they pressed up against each other on the cracked seat of his Subaru wagon, inhaling the smells of french fries, stale coffee, Dial body wash, and orange peels.

There was always, always, a new guy.

The new guy. That's how she identified them in her contacts so she wasn't changing names every other week, just phone numbers. Though this new guy was different. It wasn't just the way his eyes had gone big at the first sight of her. It was more the attention he paid to her words and moods and gestures, as if he wanted to absorb the totality of her.

She'd never been a looks girl, so she liked that he wasn't strikingly fine. His nose was mildly humped, his features were slightly asymmetrical, and he didn't have growing hair, a term her mother used, and Ayana could never figure out why that was important to Lorna. When he smiled, Ayana felt movement in the air around her as if it needed to stretch to accommodate his magnificence. He went by Moe but had confided that his given name was Most, because his mother said that he was the most she could ever ask for in a child. Ayana thought she and his mother had that in common. And his mother didn't even know what Ayana knew, that his Subaru wagon was also his dorm room. He was a senior at Penn, and living in his car enabled him to send the portion of his scholarship that covered housing back home to his mother in Mississippi to help her pay for the cost of insulin for his younger brother; he told his mother it was from a special grant so she would accept it. That type of devotion to his family told Ayana everything she needed to know about him, so she'd decided that tonight they'd consummate their relationship. But just as she was enjoying the feel of his lips against hers, there it was, a premonition that shook her.

"Shit, shit, shit," she said, and pulled back.

"Wha, I swear, I showered at the gym," he moaned as he tried to kiss her again.

"It's not you, get over yourself," she said as she sat up and straightened her clothes.

"What it is, then?"

"Family shit," she said, trying to slow her breathing to keep herself from imploding the way she sometimes did after glimpsing the future. When it was bad, she'd have to roll herself into a ball and rock and moan to try to hold on to the thousand pieces of herself, because her body felt like it was shattering from the inside out. She was fourteen the first time the aftereffects of a knowing were that severe. Her parents rushed her to the ER, and the episode was diagnosed as a panic attack, followed by a Prozac prescription. Then there was the time she'd had a premonition that a nearby apartment building would go up in flames. Over the next three days she'd gone to the building and pulled the fire alarm, and on the third day a faulty boiler exploded, igniting the building, but even the mostly students who'd assumed it was another false alarm were able to get out in time. She was eighteen when it happened again. She'd seen the sweetest kid, who lived on her great-grandmother's block, tased by the police because they thought he'd just robbed the new vegan bakery in the gentrifying neighborhood. The vision she'd just had was even worse. Now she had to get out of her new guy's car so she wouldn't subject him to the mess she was about to become before his eyes.

"You're shaking, Ayana, c'mere," he said, his voice wet with concern. "Talk to me, what kinda family shit?" He reached for her.

"I gotta go, gotta get home." Her voice screeched as she pulled away from Moe.

"Well, at least let me take you," he said.

"You do know I live right around the corner? I'm good, I'll hit you up later."

She stuffed her arms into her jacket and closed her ears to his pleas for her to stay. She was already out of the car, already running through the nighttime currents that rose and fell like high tide under the moonlight; secrets riding atop the waves created a silvery froth, rendering them less sordid. She pulled out her phone and scrolled through her contacts to C, for Cue, praying he'd pick up, and when he did, a warmth shot through her.

"Yo, 'sup," he said.

"Hey, you."

"Headed my way?"

"If I can, yeah."

"Cool, then."

And already she was walking up the three flights of stairs, through the darkened hallway that smelled of cabbage and salt pork, knocking on his door where the wood was splintered and gray. His one room was a haven for her with the space heater in the winter, the box fan in the summer, the high-backed armless chair, and the naked bed. His shoulders and mouth, his hands, his manhood and prepositions: atop, below, under, over, in, out, around and around, until she was spinning with the earth, his breath in her ear. "Another bad vision, baby?"

"Yeah," she gasped.

"Yeeaaah. Tell me."

She wrapped her arms tightly around his back and talked

in stuttered whispers, unintelligible broken sentences about what she'd seen: that sacred house built by GG's father, complete with a skylight of stained glass with an etched rainbow in honor of their ancestor Luda centered perfectly over the space in the living room. Ayana felt so pure, so exalted in that space when she gathered with them for rituals, adorned in elaborate handsewn garb, where they swayed and chanted in voices pitched high and low, where they tarried until the power of the Knowing moved among them. Then a furious bang split the house, the earth, the universe. Shattered glass spilling over her great-grandmother, her grandmother, her aunts and cousins; even her aunt Lil, who'd been banned from that house decades ago, was there, a ceiling beam falling, her aunt Lil falling.

Ayana's voice went screechy as she recalled what she'd seen.

He cradled her tighter. "I got you, baby," he said, "let it out, yeah, you wit me, you good, you good."

She then felt herself being lifted, propelled up and up and up higher, rising above her frenzied torment, until she was at the pinnacle, hollering mercy as they lasted. Now spent as she came down, gentler ebbs and flows inching her back.

✦ ✦ ✦

Morning rippled its pinks and yellows through the darkness as Ayana tiptoed along the hard dirt of the garden and climbed in through the basement window of her parents' house. She felt ridiculous, sneaking in the way she used to when she was thirteen. But after five years of trying to finish college, and now back home with her parents, she was working hard to hold to their arrangement of her taking a year off from school, getting a job, and doing some serious introspection that did not include strings of late nights.

She consistently fell short on the late nights.

She dropped down from the window into the unfinished part of the basement. She plunked on the stool and pushed her hand into the pocket of her shearling-lined denim jacket and pulled out a whopping globe-shaped cherry Tootsie Pop. She'd planned to give it to Moe because he'd told her once that sugar helped him sleep. "You's a crazy ass," she'd said, and they'd laughed for five minutes, and they hadn't even smoked any weed.

She unwrapped the lollipop and put it in her mouth. The cherry flavor coated her tongue. She bit down hard, trying to crack it open. She wanted to get to the center, Moe's favorite part, the Tootsie Roll that was gooey and sweet. The lollipop was still too firm, the softer sweetness too encased.

She replayed the image of the stained-glass rainbow falling over their ritual space, then the ceiling beam, then her aunt Lil falling. She thought about how she'd just recounted it all to Cue. How it had calmed her, but also how soiled it had made her feel.

At times like this she resented her mother for forcing her to deny her abilities, to lie to GG and the rest of the Maces, to erase for her the advantage that the other Mace women had to experience a Knowing within their sacred community, to be pampered and comforted as they verbalized what they saw. She yearned to be able to act in kind, but she feared it was too late for her, feared that her great-grandmother would see through her frail attempts at acting if a premonition was new for her. Feared GG would evict her from their lives the same way she'd done Miles's sister Lil. So all she had was Cue, who was a stranger, who essentially knew more about her than anyone else.

✦ ✦ ✦

Ayana first encountered Cue over four years ago. She was eighteen and had accompanied her cousin Bree to a birthday at a private club for one of the lawyers at the firm where Bree worked as part of her college work-study program. She and Bree were close, and Bree was her favorite cousin, partly because she wasn't bothered by the glaring favoritism GG showed to Ayana.

Ayana and Bree were having a good time buzzing from the Chablis and dancing with each other because the men there were self-congratulatory, pompous shits, so opposite from Ayana and Bree with their open personalities, freestanding crinkly hair, and panoplies of colors and fabrics in their shawls and high-low hems and sueded ankle booties even though it was seventy degrees.

She felt his eyes on her before she even noticed him. The energy from his gaze made her turn all the way around to the bar adjacent to the wall of windows that looked out on the crowded skyline above Billy Penn's statue. She couldn't tell if he worked for the law firm and was going rogue in his sneakers and jeans and Eagles jersey, or if he worked for the club and was managing the setup, or, like her, was just there with a cousin or a girlfriend or a date. It did not matter as she walked to the window and to him.

"'Sup," he said when she was close enough. His voice was deep, he was wide-chested, neither short nor tall, middle-of-the-road complexion, hair cut close, no beard, no mustache. Strikingly, though, he had green eyes, and he smelled of lavender.

"Cue," he said as he extended his hand. She met his handshake with a smile. She liked that he didn't try to squeeze or rub her hand or otherwise prolong the handshake.

"As in the letter Q?" she asked.

"As in C-U-E." He spelled it out.

"I could follow up with a half-dozen questions, like do you play pool, for starters. But I won't."

"I appreciate you for that. Especially since I don't know your name, might be possibilities there for me."

"Ayana," she said.

"Of course you'd have a perfect name. I can't even mess around with it. What's it mean?"

"Flower."

"Beautiful flower, right?"

"Why'd you ask me if you knew, then?"

"Curious if you'd leave out the 'beautiful.' I figured you would." She didn't have a reply as she looked at his nose, his mouth, his forehead. Not his eyes. She reasoned those green eyes on a Black man likely garnered more attention than they were worth. A cliché. He had a pretty mouth, though, his lips were heart-shaped, dark. But his forehead protruded. Lorna's sister maintained that people with protruding foreheads were cerebral, calculating, and would take advantage of you . . . if you let them.

Ayana didn't get that sense. In fact, she sensed him to be on a higher plane.

"You good, Ayana?" he asked, pulling her attention back to his eyes. She conceded the eyes had the potential to mesmerize.

She nodded.

"Cool, enjoy the evening," he said, then turned and walked away.

An hour later, as she stood at the sink in the bathroom washing her hands with vanilla chai soap, enjoying the smell, the errant bubbles rising from her hands and then disappearing, leaving dots of mist in their wake, it happened. The stillness happened that always preceded the mental eclipse when her literal world's orbit passed another world, imparting to her an awareness of what was to come. She never saw colors or images, never heard voices. No auras or waves moving through the air, no ringing in her ears; she just came to know something that was otherwise unknowable. A gift given. That's what her great-grandmother would say during rituals. For Ayana, who didn't have the benefit of community, of being surrounded the way the family surrounded, and rocked, and soothed whoever had just been privy to a tomorrow, the gift took as it gave. In the aftermath, she'd experience a loss of control. She felt it coming on as she stood over the sink in the club's bathroom. Her hands began to tremble, her breaths quickened. The light hit her eyes like sprays of sand. She closed her eyes and turned off the water and wiped her hands on her blouse to dry them, to attempt to still them, as she heard a toilet flush. She pushed out of the bathroom and tried not to stagger to where Bree was chatting it up with the firm's other work-study student.

"I'm sick. I'm going to Uber it home," Ayana said.

"You look like shit, I'm coming with you," Bree said.

"Hell no, you're not," Ayana said.

She wished she could say more. Wished she could pull Bree away from the center of the swanky clubroom for which they were underdressed and overly authentic and tell her that she was shaking because she'd just experienced a Knowing about a down-the-street neighbor on the block where her father grew up and where the Maces still lived after decades, an affable fourteen-year-old who'd had a crush on her since he was ten, and would always remind her that only four years separated them, that he was gonna marry her one day, and he didn't even care if she was from a family of witches—that line always made her laugh—and that he'd take on anybody who tried to mess with her; she'd just seen that lovely boy who had endeared himself to her tased by the police, around the corner from his own house no less, because the just-opened vegan bakery had been robbed and the priority was to protect the businesses and new white residents in the gentrifying neighborhood, not the innocent Black boys born there.

But she couldn't say that to Bree. She couldn't say it to anybody. She felt herself a fraud. She, who could look around the clubroom of wannabes and pride herself on being so real, could not even say to her closest cousin, whose hand she held at every ritual's opening prayer, that she was about to implode because she knew that the most lovable boy was going to be left paralyzed by police whose explicit bias was too entrenched for even the heaviest concentrations of diversity training to cure.

"Well, I don't need GG kicking my ass if something should happen to you," Bree said, concern crinkling her heavily mascaraed brows. "I'm at least going down with you and watch you get into the Uber—"

"I'm okay." She cut Bree off as she pulled her in a hug. It was a long hug because her cousin wouldn't let go.

✦ ✦ ✦

The cool breeze buzzed through the dark blue air over Market Street after she'd left Bree at the party in the clubroom. Ayana was both hot and cold standing on that corner, both damp with sweat and chilled to the point of shaking. Her heart thumped triple-time from the sensory overload out there: the whoosh of car tires and horns and people laughing and talking in the loudest voices; the bombardment of lights, so many lights, their shapes and colors magnified into outsize blobs. The smells of steak fat and car exhaust, aftershave, garlic, wine were crowding her nose and throat and chest. She tried to get to the bottom of her purse for her phone to order the Uber. She couldn't still her hands enough to grab her phone. She leaned against the light pole. She wanted to slide down to the pavement and curl up in a ball and rock herself.

She heard a siren stop in front of her then. She thought maybe some Good Samaritan had observed her distress and called 911 on her behalf. But it wasn't a siren. It was tires screeching with a pitch so intense that it sounded like a scream. She closed her eyes to the blinding luminescence of headlights coming right at her. Another car's tires screamed, a horn blared, and she thought there would be a collision. A door slammed. An argument. Testosterone rolled like thunder:

"Come on, man, really? What the fuck, you just goin' stop short like that?"

"Man, shut up and wait a minute."

"No, you move that fucking truck right now."

"I said wait a minute, asshole." And she recognized the voice, the familiar gruffness getting closer, so close that she could smell the lavender seeming to cling to his breath as he whispered to her closed eyes, "Ayana, you need help? You need me to drop you somewhere? I'll take you home? To the ER? Tell me what you need."

She nodded, then managed to say yes to nothing specific, just yes.

He wrapped his arms around her shoulders and guided her to his truck and strapped her into the seat. She leaned forward and rubbed her hands up and down her arms and tried to swallow the urge to vomit. "Uh, I might spit up," she said, gasping. "I'm sorry."

He pulled off from the corner. "You're good," he said. "I'll pull over if I have to. Where you wanna go, the ER? Jeff is the closest."

"No," she said.

"I'll take you home, then; where you live?"

"No, no."

"Cool, well, tell me where."

She hunched her shoulders.

"What you coming off of? Fentanyl?" he asked.

"It's not like that."

"What's it like, then?"

"This just happens sometimes."

"Just happens? You got a lot going on there for just happens. The shakes, the sweats, I bet your heart's racing. Your heart racing?"

She didn't answer as she continued to rub her hands up and down her arms. She felt a blast of heat as he angled the vents toward her.

"Cool, we'll just drive, then," he said.

They were leaving Center City as he turned onto Kelly Drive.

She was still hypersensitive to sights and sounds, but at least the inside of his truck was quiet compared to Market Street. Her skin still itched, crawled, as if trying to pull away from her flesh and bones. But she noticed that the points where he had pressed against her shoulders and her arm and her wrist to help her into the truck were calm, soothed. She was still shaking and sweating, but slightly less, and the urge to vomit had passed.

"You not twitching as much," he said, as if he'd read her mind. "I can make you some tea when we get to my crib. You like tea?"

She nodded.

"You okay going to my crib? It's right on Lincoln Drive, so easy enough for you to leave if you wanna leave."

She didn't respond. "I guess silence is consensus," he said. "Cool?"

"I see shit," she said then.

He kept looking straight ahead, as though he knew that if he turned his eyes on her, she'd swallow the rest of what she was trying to say. "And then this happens." She stopped so she could catch her breath, and she was also starting to cry.

"Okay, so you see shit, to use your word, 'cause I don't usually curse in front of women I don't know. Can I ask, what kind of shit do you see?"

She covered her face with her hands, not believing those words had come from her.

"Like what? Delusionary shit, uh, stuff that's not there?" he pressed.

"Not there yet," she said.

"Not there yet? Okay?" They drove in silence for minutes. Then he said more than asked: "So you see future shit."

"Yeah."

"Tragedies?"

"Sometimes."

"Damn, okay, and the shit, uh, stuff you see ever come true?"

"Yeah," she said, her voice sudsy now.

He let out a long, loud exhale. "Okay," he said, and after another pause added, "Well, at least it's not fentanyl."

He was turning into a parking lot on Lincoln Drive, and

they were walking through a lobby that had once been grand, with its spiral staircase and domed ceiling and marble flooring, but, with a little dressing up, was now more apt for the setting of a haunted house. She was dizzy and still had the shakes, so her gait was halting, off balance, and he offered to carry her up the three flights of stairs. "No," she said as she reached for the wide, curved banister.

"Cool, 'cause I wouldn't want my neighbors to think I eloped and was carrying my bride over the threshold. I wonder if people still do that. You think people still do that?"

She didn't answer as she concentrated on navigating the stairs. He walked closely behind her. "I got you if you fall," he said. "Otherwise, keeping my hands to myself." She knew that he would. She'd always had a heightened sense about a person's intentions, whether they meant her harm or ill will. It was how she'd kept herself safe with men.

They walked through a door with scraped wood into a living room and kitchen combined. A couch, a chair, a bed. She sat on the bed and shivered. He stood next to the bed.

"I'll heat water for tea. You ready for some tea? I got herbal, Earl Grey, but the Grey might keep you hyped. How about some chamomile?"

"No tea," she said.

"Cool, no tea. Uh, you mind if I sit next to you? I can go sit on the couch if you prefer. You can, too, if you want. Couch is more comfortable."

She hunched her shoulders as if it didn't matter where he sat. Though she truly did want him next to her. His touch had calmed the places on her skin where his fingers pressed when he'd led her to his truck. It was as if he had healing powers, like GG's sister Helene claimed that she did, or like the preachers who did the laying on of hands. She shifted ever so slightly as if inviting him to sit next to her. He did, stiffly at first.

"You wanna tell me what you saw that's not real yet that's got you melting down like this? It's cool if not, but it might help. I promise I won't think you're crazy. But lemme ask, are you crazy? If you not crazy, and just got powers, you not gonna put a spell on me, are you? My aunt was into that. My mom would never comb her hair at my aunt's house 'cause she said if my aunt gotta hold of a strand of your hair, and was mad at you for some reason, she could hex you and have you crawling on your belly."

He let out a chuckle that hung in midair, unfinished, because she'd just picked up his hand and pressed it against her cheek. He made a sound from the back of his throat and stroked her cheek with his fingers. His touch was velvet.

"You've got beautiful skin," he said as she guided his hand to her chin, her throat, her collarbone, as she half babbled, half cried about the boy who had a crush on her and what the police were going to do to him.

He took her home after that first time. She nestled in the silence of his truck. She'd been with several men by eighteen. All fairly meaningless encounters. She didn't berate or judge herself for it. She didn't broadcast her escapades. Sometimes she'd tell Bree if the tryst was remarkable in any way. Generally, they were not. This encounter with Cue, though, had been remarkable. Beyond the fire, there was the unexpected peace afterward resulting from having a cavernous craving satisfied: She'd actually described the substance of a Knowing to another human being. She'd done that only one other time, when she'd whispered in the ear of the elderly lady on the mobility scooter in front of Marshalls that day and told her the red car would crash through the window. She was just a little girl and thought it was normal, thought that everybody from time to time knew a thing would happen before it happened.

The resettling of her mind and body into all the appropriate places was stunning as Cue drove her home after that first time. And every time since.

✦ ✦ ✦

Like now, as she sat in the dusty unfinished part of her parents' basement, sucking on the lollipop she'd bought for Moe to consummate their relationship. Instead, she'd run from his car to find relief with Cue.

The harder she sucked on the lollipop, the more unavailable to her the softer, sweeter center became. She pulled it from her mouth and put it under her sneaker and stomped it with her heel until it shattered. She watched flecks of red mix with the dust particles twirling on the bands of new-day light. She slipped out of her shearling-lined denim jacket and covered her face with the jacket so its softness would meet her hard sobs. Then she cried.

Salvation

July 2019, Nona's Writing Room, Philadelphia Exurbs

Nona could feel Ayana's sobs moving through her own chest as she got up from her desk to start dinner for Bob, her husband. Generally she'd remain with a scene like the one that had just pulled her in so deeply that she had the shakes herself as she wrote it, and was herself inhaling the dust in the basement, and covering herself with the shearling-lined denim jacket (the jacket no doubt given to Ayana by fashion-conscious Lorna), trying to soften the mean vibrations in her rib cage as the sobs moved through.

She extricated herself from the writing, though, to cook dinner for Bob because it was his first night home after piloting a string of flights that had kept him on the road, or in the air, as it were, for long stretches. She thought he deserved some real nutrition after streams of airline food, restaurant food, food-court food, microwavable hotel food. Whatever else kind of food from God knew where.

She prepped halibut for baking. The fish was soft and sleek under her fingers as she rubbed it down with olive oil and sprinkled coarse salt over the fillet and gently pressed the crystals into the halibut's tender skin. She thought about Ayana. Wondered what really had made Ayana cry. Wondered if she'd felt shame for jumping out of her new guy's car to rush to Moe.

Nona thought about her own years-ago self, her shameless self. She'd joke with her girlfriends about how there had been no shame to her game when she was young. "Shit was fun. I had hips like Nicki Minaj. Please, had it not been for Bob, I might still be out there."

She lied about the fun part. It was not. She was angry at her mother for dying on her, her father for abandoning her by giving her to his sister, so she retaliated by living a worse version of herself.

She met Bob during undergrad. They sat across the table from each other in a survey course on Romantic poets. She winked at him during a debate about what Coleridge was saying in "Dejection." After class, he extended his hand and formally introduced himself. She invited him back to her dorm room. He insisted on coffee across the street instead, explaining that he was a member of the Black Jesus Campus Crusaders—all the members were Black, and they believed that Jesus was Black, too.

Nona declined his offer for coffee; she wasn't interested in hearing more about his Black Campus Crusade group. Not that she didn't also love a Black Jesus, but she wasn't about to blow her own or anyone else's high by proselytizing about how the wages of sin are death as she smoked weed and opium and dropped tabs of acid, drank cheap fruity wine, got down with one boy after the next, after the next. So many boys, so many different beds, or chairs, or floors. So much numbness to work toward. So much to unfeel.

She and Bob managed to become friends during the span of the course. Both with lines drawn: He wouldn't try to convert her; she wouldn't try to get him aroused.

Several years later, well into her twenties and working as a paralegal after taking a break from law school, she was running through O'Hare Airport, clad in a miniskirt and cropped T-shirt, braless, lipstick smeared, hair pulled every which way as if she'd just been with the driver in the back of the Quicky airport transport van, which she had.

She heard Bob's voice behind her then, whispering in her ear. "You're so much better than this, Nona."

She turned, and there he was in his crisp pilot's uniform, gold wing on his lapel. An endless blue sky rushed through the airport's windowed walls as if it had delivered him there to stand behind her and whisper in her ear.

He looked down on her—not in a judgmental way, though, he was just tall. He took off his pilot's cap; his flock of curls courtesy of the blend of his Mexican mother and Jamaican father had been cut way close, just waves now. His soft boyish features had grown into manhood, his complexion more reddened, more robust. He was beautiful. She felt a chill that came not from the air around her but from inside her. She began to shake, near convulsively. In that instant she was experiencing something she never had. Shame.

She wondered if he could see her shame as his face opened in concern and he took her hand and led her closer to the sky-drenched window.

He took off his pilot's jacket with the angelic gold wings and wrapped it around her and rubbed his hands up and down her arms to warm her. "You know Jesus loves you, Nona. He loves you especially. And so do I." He asked her then if she wanted salvation. "Right here, right now. If you simply confess with your mouth and believe in your heart, you will be saved."

The following week Nona cleared her South Street efficiency of all the bongs, Top paper, hash pipes, condoms. She unplugged her phone and answering machine. She bought a cookbook and learned how to make halibut. It became their special dish over the years, and even now she prepared it for him on his first night home.

He walked in the kitchen and grabbed her by the waist. She leaned back into his arms, and he rubbed her stomach in gentle circles. He'd just showered. A minty scent rose from his skin and wrapped them up, twisting around and around them like a destructive cyclone preparing for landfall over an idyllic island retreat. She realized then that the reason Ayana was crying into the soft lining of the jacket had nothing to do with shame. She did what she had to do to give herself relief. Like Nona had, too. Ayana was crying because of her awareness of the awfulness to come.

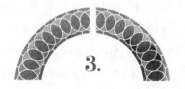

3.
Surprise Guests

It had been several weeks since Ayana had experienced the traumatic Knowing when she'd seen her great-grandmother's house demolished, her aunt Lil on the floor like a splendid oak felled. She was managing to shutter the vision, to starve it of light and air, by concentrating instead on what she was doing in the moment; when she couldn't sustain that, she'd remind herself that the foretelling could not come to fruition without Lil's presence in that house, which was unlikely after the decades-ago upheaval that had stormed through the family like Katrina, breaching levees and alliances. Lil never returned to Philadelphia, though she did remain close with her older sister, Bev, and Miles, her younger brother and Ayana's father.

Bev and Lil had helped raise Miles. Their mother, Hortense, was exhausted by the time her son came along. By then Bev and Lil were already in their teens, and Hortense was looking forward to their total self-sufficiency. But to her disappointment, she found herself pregnant, depressed, burdened. As GG's only child, Hortense was tasked with helping to run the business. Though the Maces were steeped in spirituality and honored their calling, which they believed stemmed from God and the ancestors, their Knowing practice also generated income. GG was the oldest, which made her the de facto CEO. Hortense and Thad, her husband, and their children lived in the storied Mace family house, so there was no escape for Hortense from duties large and small, which included prepping for the rituals and the after-feasts, managing the books, scheduling appointments, doling out house-fix-up duties for the men: The house was old, and systems constantly stalled, or choked, or broke altogether.

Hortense dragged herself through the nine months with her swollen feet, her back spasms, her heartburn, Miles kicking her from the inside like drumrolls meant to prepare her for what she already knew, responsibility so large it would barely fit in her arms. She cried every night. Thad held her, massaged her back and her feet, comforted her as he could when he wasn't on the road yet again for weeks-long assignments for his government job landing him in Colorado, or New Mexico, or Portland; always far-flung places; rarely DC or Maryland or Virginia. The extended Mace family's curiosity about Thad's travels rippled with insinuation. "Where he going now? For how long this time? That far?" one of the aunts would remark with a side-eye to the others as they spread around the expansive maple table for the post-ritual feast.

Bev, the most outspoken of Hortense's offspring, would rush to defend her father, saying something like "Thank God for his good government job, you know how much it costs to keep this old house up to code?" She'd mention his latest undertakings, like the new roof he'd just had put on, or the addition he'd had built that extended to the back of the house beyond the kitchen to accommodate family sleeping over when they wanted, or having new electrical panels installed and the house rewired.

But despite all that Thad did, he was often unavailable, and Hortense was tired, the kind of tired that sucked at even the energy it took to feel a little joy. Certainly too tired to have a baby sucking on her around the clock. So she swaddled Miles in the softest blankets from the many that the aunts and cousins had crocheted, she held him to her heart and kissed his forehead, she heated his baby formula to the perfect temperature, then she alternated between Bev and Lil every evening, rolling his bassinet into their room. "He's yours for the night," she'd say. Bev and Lil lapped up the responsibility, loving on Miles as if he were their very own doll baby. Hortense would return to her own silent room, snuggle up with the pillow where her husband's head should be, and fall into a sleep so sound, she felt like she was dying every night.

A few years later, Lil committed what GG considered an unforgivable offense. GG not only banned Lil from the house but forbade even the mention of Lil's name in her presence. Most of the family acquiesced to GG; even Lil's own mother took GG's side.

However, Bev, and Thad, and, by default, Miles, who was too young to know what was going on, but certainly would have chosen Lil anyhow, remained loyal to Lil.

From as far back as Ayana could remember, she and her parents visited with Lil at least once a year, when Lil's world-spanning travels brought her nearby. In December, when Lil touched down to attend holiday gatherings hosted by her publisher, her agents, her friends in the entertainment industry, Ayana and her parents took the train into New York. Lil had been a media darling in her younger days, and her royalty statements and consultant fees still gained her entrée into the exclusive soirees.

Lil would cry hard and openly when she'd meet them at Penn Station. She'd grab Miles and hold on. Then she'd open her arms to Lorna, whom she called sweetness, which, when Ayana was a young child, made her squinch her face in confusion—Ayana thought her mother many things but rarely thought her sweet. Lorna would gush as Lil complimented her hair or outfit, or said how grateful she was that her baby brother had such a phenomenal wife. Then Lil would focus on Ayana. She'd cup her chin and peer so deeply into her eyes that something inside Ayana would shift and she'd experience a rare sense of okayness, wholeness, that she only felt when she chanted and swayed with her family during rituals. It was as if her aunt's gaze lit a path all the way to her core and found even the most imperfect parts of her worthy. She couldn't fathom what had made GG excise Lil the way she had. She resisted asking her mother when she'd last heard from Lil. Sometimes she found peace in the unknowing.

Family Spirit

Ayana's adjustment from her college campus apartment back to her childhood bedroom had been a torment. Twenty-two years old and no degree, no plan, no accomplishments; her parents arguing about money, reminding her how much her college tuition had drained them; her mother's constant updates on church members, or sorority members, or neighborhood folk whose daughters were headed to Penn Law, or Howard Med, or MSW, PhysD, MFA, SLP, MBA programs, so many letters from here to perpetuity. Even her cousins, the great-granddaughters of GG's sisters, were showing off their wingspans, preparing to soar. No soaring for Ayana. Only the nest she'd returned to with its protruding twigs scraping the skin on her back, leaving it welted and raw.

She thought that part of her unexplained contentment came from her new job. She'd quit Starbucks and was now working for a West Philly coffee shop that was decadently upscale for Fifty-Second Street. The owners' hope was that the Penn students would walk through their fear of traveling west of Forty-Fourth and get a dose of African Arabica medium roast sweetened with real city life. Ayana's hope was for the indigenous residents; she wanted them to experience the sublime taste of her perfectly prepared cup of pour-over coffee, or an espresso shot, or her lattes that would put Starbucks's to shame. She persuaded the owners to offer free coffee tastings two mornings a week from six until seven. She informed the locals that they could use their SNAP/EBT benefits for the zucchini bread, the fruit cups. She endeared herself to the older patrons, like Miss Dot with the silver-blue hair that was always freshly pressed and curled. Miss Dot had a theatrical style, especially when she talked about the nightclubs that once lined the Strip, the mile-long limos depositing the famous. The acts that performed. "Baby girl, let me tell you," she'd say. "We didn't have to go to no New York to boogaloo down Broadway, we had our own Broadway right here." She'd punctuate her words with a shimmy of her hips and high fives to any of her contemporaries who might be nearby.

Ayana would call Moe to wake him early on those free-coffee mornings so he could get his complimentary cup and mingle with the people.

She watched Moe walk into the café now and felt the surge that always moved through her when she first saw him, even before he brightened the space around him with his smile, giving the space a burst of warmth and goodness.

"Hey, you," she said, unable to contain her cheeks rounding out in a blush.

He pursed his mouth and blew her a kiss. His eyes were caked with sleep, and were it not a health violation, she would have reached over the counter and gently wiped away the bits of crust from the corners of his eyes the way she did in the mornings when they woke together in the back of his Subaru. She handed him a napkin and gestured toward his eyes.

"Oh, thanks," he said as he adjusted his backpack and wiped his eyes. "I crashed at my frat's crib last night," he leaned over the counter to whisper, "and ended up playing pinochle half the night, so your wake-up call was so on time."

"You know I be looking out." She winked and poured his coffee.

"You know I be looking at you," he said, and gave up the smile that made her swoon.

Miss Dot called out to him from her regular seat at the corner table that caught the morning sun angling through the coated windows. "Hey there, cute young boy"—her other name for Moe—"get over here and let me finish up my story from last time."

"You better go get your history on," Ayana said to him as she handed him his coffee over the counter, "or it's gonna be some shit in here." He laughed and blew her another kiss and told Miss Dot he was just gonna grab some cream for his java and he'd be right there. He angled his cup and nodded and said what's up as he walked past the man standing behind him.

"'Sup," the man replied, and Ayana felt a jolt in her stomach. She didn't have to look up to confirm that it was Cue because the sound of his voice was embedded in the part of her brain that processed such things, and tucked in the pouch that held her emotional responses. She didn't know at first how to respond to this man with whom she had a—a what? A relationship? She couldn't even call it that because it was too amorphous, too shapeless, to define. Nor did she ever desire to define it, to pin it down, to pin them down into an unsustainable conventionality. She knew nothing about him, where he worked, if he worked, if he had a family, friends, if he even lived in the bare room she'd frequent infrequently. She didn't need to know, didn't want to know. All she understood was that being with him in the immediate aftermath of a traumatic Knowing—the way she'd been with him those few weeks ago when she'd run from Moe's car after having the awareness that the top of GG's house would come crashing down, her aunt Lil absorbing the worst of it—saved her from the agony, the mania, the loss of control. But that was the extent of it, of what, their togetherness? Yes, the full extent; she was with Moe, after all. Wanted to be with Moe. Just Moe.

But now he was standing in front of her, and her wants turned topsy-turvy like her stomach. She concentrated on her feet, pushed them farther into the floor to root her, to help her stand straight, still, without moving back and forth like a laughable bobblehead of herself. She locked her dark eyes on his green ones as he stood where he should never be, in front of her in public, in the light of day, at her workplace. She never considered his eyes when she thought about him after they'd been together. She considered his arms, his chest, his hold on her that lingered. She shook her shoulders now as if shaking off the feel of his arms. "Good morning, what can I get for you?" she heard her voice squeak.

"I'll have whatever you just fixed for the good brother over there." He motioned toward Moe.

"Regular coffee?"

"It's free till eight, right?"

"Actually seven," she said. Managing to keep her voice steady. Managing not to ask him what the fuck was he doing walking in here this morning, breaking their unspoken rule, well, maybe not a rule but at least a pattern they'd stuck to over the past four years, which had sustained them because they'd respected the pattern, or whatever it was that had no name, no shape, that still guided their behavior: She called him when the need arose, not desire, she convinced herself, need. And if he answered, he'd always answered, she'd rush to him for her relief. That was it, he relieved her. And in return, he got what he got, his satisfaction, in equal measure. But now he was here, in this café, outside of the pattern that had been sustained with invisible ink, which they respected even more because they couldn't see the lines they'd drawn.

She'd never told him where she worked. Had he searched her out through her cell phone number? Had he stalked her? Had he known Moe was here and so he'd decided to just breeze on in to fuck with her?

She decided that the only way she could respond would be to look him in his eyes and act normal. But even normal felt like an abstraction in this moment, when she was working hard not to display on the outside what she was feeling: that she was petrified Moe would detect the energy between them, because that energy had its own force field, and Ayana didn't know how to disrupt it.

"Regular coffee is good," he said. His face was neutral. "Are you?"

"Am I what?" she asked, off to the side, pouring his coffee. "Good?"

"So good," she said, allowing a drop of sarcasm to her tone. "Your first time here?"

"It is, yeah."

"How'd you hear about us?"

"My boy hipped me. He's showing through in a minute. Said the barista here makes a helluva cuppa."

She was back in front of him, working to keep her hands steady as she pushed a sleeve up onto the cup. He was wearing a tan tweed jacket over a navy T-shirt. She'd never seen him in the light of day. His mild complexion was smooth, blemish-free. His round face had a boyish innocence. Was the innocence new, or had it been there all along?

Miss Dot was saying something that made Moe explode with laughter. Ayana loved the sound of Moe's laughter, which boomed from a deep place, giving it a righteous quality.

"Seems like a cool dude," Cue said, motioning to Moe.

"The coolest," Ayana said, handing him his coffee.

He took the coffee and nodded and said thank you, then paused and cleared his throat as if he wanted to say more. Ayana held his gaze, held her breath, held her stomach muscles tightly.

"It's cool," he said then. "No worries. You're good." He turned and walked toward the side of the café opposite where Moe and Miss Dot sat chatting. Miss Dot and Moe were no longer laughing as Moe leaned in, listening intently to whatever story Miss Dot was telling, apparently a gripping tale to judge by the mishmash expression on Moe's face, his eyebrows meeting in the middle, his forehead creased, his mouth shaped like the letter O. Ayana was relieved that Moe was not focused on her or Cue.

She allowed her own chest to release the breaths she'd been holding; she untensed her stomach, her back, her knees, parts of her body that she'd not even been aware she was constricting. The timer beeped and she dumped the coffee grinds and began her prep for the soon-to-arrive paying customers. She swallowed the suds in her throat that were trying to move up, trying to make her cry.

A half hour later and Cue was still sipping his coffee at the café table, alone. His so-called boy hadn't shown, and Ayana wondered if it was all a lie. Moe was preparing to leave. He put on his Old Navy sweat jacket and affixed his backpack over his shoulders and walked to her counter and leaned in and told her he'd see her later. His breath was warm and smelled of heated milk, such a calming aroma. She smiled and pursed her lips and gave him an air kiss. She watched him leave, determined not to look at Cue to see if he was watching him, too, or her. Moe was tall and lean and had a smooth walk for a country boy, walked as if he knew the streets. He didn't, though. His innocence both charmed and frightened her.

She glanced at the clock. She hit the bell on her counter. "Last call for complimentary coffee," she said. She went into the back to get more half-and-half from the fridge. She lined up plastic condiment containers and filled each with milk, or cream, or skim milk, then put them in the appropriate ice-laden bowls on the stand with the coffee lids, sugar, and plasticware. She always put out more than necessary and turned her head when people slipped extras in their totes or pockets. That was how she'd met Moe. At her old job, she'd noticed him stuffing his backpack with spoons, napkins, whatever was out. One day during lull time, as he sat in the corner tapping away on his computer, she called out to him, "Sir, I think this is yours," as she walked over to him and set down a paper plate holding a healthy slice of lemon pound cake. He read her expression, which said, *Go with me on this one, please.* His confusion melted into a smile that still touched her heart. Not just now, though. Just now she felt too soiled with Moe and Cue occupying the same space in the café, even as she tried to tell herself that her time with Cue was . . . what? She didn't even know what it was.

The door opened, and she looked up and saw a woman walking in, smiling so wide that her face could barely contain the smile. Ayana's first thought was *Damn, she has a smile just like Aunt Bev,* though her aunt Bev generally didn't open her face like this woman; Bev more often smirked than smiled. Plus, Bev was not nearly as stylish as this woman in cropped boot-cut jeans and a wool poncho in muted red and orange, with a tan slouchy hat with a red fur ball.

Then Ayana gasped when she realized who it was. "My God," she squealed as she ran from behind the counter to meet the arms wide open for her. "Is this really you?" she asked. "Aunt Lil, is this you? Here, in Philly. You're actually here in Philly."

She poured herself into Lil's arms. She was both elated because her aunt was here and devastated because Lil being here meant the alignment toward her Knowing had begun. She was both crushed by the thought of harm coming to her aunt and exalted by the way her aunt's presence lifted her higher than the messiest impressions she had of herself. She rested her head on Lil's shoulder, laughing and crying. "Aunt Lil," she said over and over, "I can't believe this is really you."

"Well, I'll take this reception any day of the week," Lil said as she rocked Ayana in her arms. "And I'm just gonna assume those are happy tears, right?"

✦ ✦ ✦

Lil was glad that Miles had dropped her at the coffee shop before taking her to his house. She needed an interim landing spot before she moved in with Miles and Lorna and Ayana, where she'd be for at least the next six weeks. She knew that Miles and Lorna would pamper her beyond their means; Lorna would have her sleeping on Frette sheets that likely broke the bank, and would try to serve her caviar, truffles, Wagyu Kobe. The attention would only remind her that although she was back in Philadelphia, she was not staying a mere few miles away in the house where she was raised, where her sister, mother, and grandmother would shun the extravagance, though the JCPenney sheets would have a silky feel, and no caviar for sure, but Bev's salmon would be restaurant quality.

She'd burned that house to the ground, though. The house still stood on that hill in Southwest Philly, still mostly served as a pulsing, welcoming harbor the way the best houses did. But not for Lil. For Lil that house was a mammoth pile of ash. She'd often wondered whether, if she poked deep into the ash, she could find a glow of possibility, of rebirth, dare she even imagine reconciliation amid the rubble. The result either way would break her heart all over again.

"I need coffee, but damn the line," she'd said to Miles at the airport as they walked toward baggage claim.

"You're in luck, big sis," he'd said. "Yanna works at a new café on Fifty-Second Street, if you can believe it." He offered to take Lil there, said he'd drop her off and then go back to the airport to get her bags. "We wanted to surprise Yanna that you were coming, and this is even better than her getting home and finding you there."

"You know, sometimes you're worth all those diapers of yours I changed," Lil had said as she watched his face round out in the signature Mace smile that was so wide and gushy and pure.

"Oh my God, I can't believe this," Ayana said now, her eyes red from crying. "I can't believe my parents held this from me. That you were actually coming to Philly, actually staying with us. Oh my God."

"Come on, now, you're gonna make me cry, and I don't cry pretty like you," Lil said, reaching in her purse for a tissue. "Every time your mother sends me a picture of you, she says how much alike we look. My reply is that I have never been cute as you, even back in the day when I was a little cute."

"You still cute, honey," Miss Dot called from her window seat as she unfolded her *Philadelphia Tribune*.

Lil twirled her index finger and laughed, then dabbed Ayana's eyes and told her she better get back behind that counter before she lost her job. "Plus, I'm seriously jonesing for a cup of your strongest brew."

"She makes the best," Miss Dot said. Her newspaper now spread out over the entire table, her magnifying glass moving across the page. "Though I think you missed the cutoff, 'cause it's no longer free."

"No worries, I'm sure it's worth whatever I have to pay," Lil said, walking away from the counter, deciding where she would sit. Deciding not to intrude on Dot's reading space, or the young white couple leaning into each other, or the girlfriends cooing over the baby in the carrier atop the table, the solo acts tapping on computers or phones or tablets. She really wanted to sit at the table where the man in the tan tweed jacket sat now. She was curious about him. He'd pretended not to be interested in Lil and Ayana's reunion, but Lil could see he was inhaling it all so completely that it quickened his breaths. She'd long ago mastered the ability to look straight ahead while still being fully cognizant of what was on either side of her, above and below. GG used to tell her that the details in the periphery were as important as the main thing; because they weren't trying to hide or embellish, they spoke the truth, if she could listen, hear. When Lil was a teen, GG had shown her a Polaroid of a young couple of seekers she was considering taking on—GG always referred to the people they helped as seekers, not clients, to downplay the business aspect of their practice. The couple needed to know if they should try to have another baby. Their first was devastatingly stricken with sickle cell disease, even though neither had the trait. They didn't want to chance bringing another child into the world to live a life of such torturous pain. GG handed Lil a photo of the couple, saying that she'd instructed them to smile. "What do you see?" she'd asked Lil. Lil told her grandmother that the husband was managing to smile, but not the wife. "Okay, look at everything about them except their mouths," GG instructed. "There are the facts that you see directly; then there is the truth that isn't always so apparent." Lil studied the photo, noticed that the husband's eyes were downcast, giving them a quality of sadness; his cheeks appeared hollowed. The wife's eyes crinkled at the corners; her cheeks were rounded like a ripening berry trying not to burst. Lil told her grandmother what she saw in the photo. "What might that mean?" GG asked. Lil said that she wasn't sure, and her grandmother told her to hold it all in her mind. "You don't have to ponder or worry over it, just let it rest. When the truth is ready, and when you are, it will speak to you."

Lil did as her grandmother instructed. It spoke to her in the middle of the night, and she ran into GG's room. GG sat up immediately, calmly, and switched on her bedside lamp as if expecting her. Lil's grandfather snored blissfully next to her.

"The baby with sickle cell is not the husband's child," Lil said to GG, gasping.

"How do you know?"

"For one, neither have the trait. That's the fact. But the truth is that the wife is too happy, like someone in love who's trying not to let it show."

GG nodded.

"So if they have another child, and if the husband is the father this time, the baby will likely be sickle cell–free." Lil had rushed her words as she watched the dim light illuminate her grandmother's eyes, shining with approval.

Lil now wondered what the truth would tell her about this man as she touched the back of the chair facing Cue. "May I?" she asked.

Family Spirit

Ayana almost spilled the coffee she was pouring as she called out, "Oh, Aunt Lil, I think he was expecting someone?"

"It's cool," Cue said as he stood and pulled the chair out for Lil. She sat, and Cue helped her push the chair closer in to the table.

"Oh my, so they still do this in Philly, or is it 'cause I'm old?"

"Chile, please," Miss Dot called without looking up from her *Tribune*. "You could still run barefoot if you wanted to. You just getting started."

The entire café laughed; even Cue laughed. Ayana didn't laugh, though, as she set her aunt's coffee down in front of her. She cut her eyes at Cue, but he was focused on his tablet, or at least she thought he pretended to be. Her breath caught in her throat, and she made a sound that was half belch, half hiccup, and both Lil and Cue looked up at her. She said excuse me and tried to make a joke about how she needed to lay off the bubbles from the milk foamer. And since Cue's eyes were on her, she said, "Sir, you are seated across from one of this world's most special people, my aunt Lil." There was a pleading to her tone that she hadn't intended.

"Yeah, I did manage to pick that up," Cue said, looking at Ayana as if seeing her for the first time. "And I'm Cue," he said to Lil, his attention still on Ayana, though.

Lil watched him watching Ayana. Noticed how his eyes softened when he looked at her. "How long have you two known each other?" Lil asked.

"Barely," Ayana blurted, then rushed back to the counter.

"I asked how long, not how well," Lil said to Cue, raising one eyebrow.

"I'm sure she meant she barely knows me, so the length of time doesn't matter," Cue said, and Lil could see he was trying to contain a smile.

Lil went right in on his eyes. "I wonder how having such a striking feature informs one's personality," she said. He looked at her with a question mark on his face as she sipped her coffee and then called out to Ayana, "Perfecto, darling." She turned back to Cue and finished her thought. "Green eyes are an anomaly, and yours are striking. And when anyone looks at you, that's the first thing they notice. And I was just wondering if that makes you feel special. Of course, you are special"—she smiled her ingratiating smile—"every person is. But what do you think?"

"You know, Aunt Lil," he said, as naturally as if he'd known her for years, though when he said that, Ayana dropped the metal filter she was cleaning into the metal sink, and the metal-on-metal bang reverberated through the café. Lil tried to suppress a laugh at her niece's endearing nervousness. She liked that he'd called her Aunt Lil. "If I had spent half my life with brown eyes," Cue continued, "I could give you an answer. I could say life was like this when they weren't green, and now that they are, it's like this. You get me?"

"I do," she said. "So you been walking around with green-eyed privilege."

"Ouch," he said, and a pained expression took over his face.

"Right? Fair-minded people hate to think they have advantages they're not aware of."

"For real, not like a skill that you work to master and rightfully take credit for the work."

"I hear you. Almost makes you want to walk around with your eyes closed."

"Or you can get contact lenses in different colors," Miss Dot called out, and snickers rippled through the café at how she wasn't even pretending not to be eavesdropping, as everyone else was.

"Are you in sales?" Lil asked. "That could cut both ways, because people are wired to mistrust salespeople, so they might consider your look all part of them being gamed."

"No, ma'am, I work in housing development."

"Uh-oh. On whose side, the people's or the exploiters'? I only ask because on the ride over, my gosh, I'm just back from Europe, where I've lived off and on for decades, and let me tell you, the changes to the neighborhoods are astounding."

Cue smiled. "I work for a community-based affordable housing entity," he said, and then couldn't say more because Miles pushed into the café.

"Oh, here's my wonderful brother, Miles," Lil said, jumping up to hug him. "Kind enough to drop me here, then go all the way back to the airport to baggage claim for my luggage, giving me the opportunity to enjoy a splendid cup of coffee and equally splendid chat with Ayana's acquaintance."

Cue stood quickly and cleared his throat and extended his hand. "Mr. Miles, Cue, nice to meet you."

"And who are you, Cue?" Miles asked as he shook Cue's hand.

"I'm just a person," Cue said.

"Well, as long as you're just a person," Miles said.

Ayana disappeared into the stockroom, thinking that her father had been around her mother too long, because that was in her playbook, make people as uncomfortable as possible. And they wondered why she never brought people around.

Jalicia, her shift-mate, arrived through the back entrance, and Ayana said she was going to slip out and get some air.

"You okay?" Jalicia asked.

"I'm good, just family drama; my dad's out there third-degreeing a guy I barely know as if he just proposed."

"Do what you gotta do, girl. I'm here," Jalicia said as she double-tied her apron and pushed through the door into the café. And Ayana could hear Miss Dot telling Lil goodbye, saying, "Remember, baby, you not old yet, you just getting started."

Ayana walked around to the front of the café as her father and aunt were getting into the car. "I'm so glad you'll be there when I get home, Aunt Lil," she said, and she leaned in to peck her cheek. "Nice to have someone special to come home to."

"Watch it, daughter," Miles said. "I'mma tell your mother on you."

"How you know it wasn't intended for you, too, Mr. *'And who are you?'*" She imitated her father's voice, and she could still hear him laughing after he pulled off and even all the way to the end of the block.

She walked to the corner and around it and back to stretch her legs. The sun was fully out, and the air was pink and blue and landed in a purple haze against the café window. She looked through the haze and blinked and said to herself, "Well, I'll be damned." The person Cue was there to meet had shown up. He was an older man with salt-and-pepper hair and a quality tan jacket that looked like cashmere. He was drinking espresso. The regulars rarely drank espresso. He and Cue were poring over Cue's tablet, their heads leaned in close.

Ayana was more curious about Cue now, what he did, how he sustained himself, as her father had just asked, who he was. She'd never been curious about the details of him before. The amorphous, shapeless nature of their relationship paradoxically could not accommodate curiosity. That had all changed. He'd initiated it by coming to her first.

He looked up as if he sensed her presence on the other side of the window. She watched him push back from the table and stand up and walk toward the door. He was next to her now. She could feel the heat of him as if he were already surrounding her. Though he wasn't. He kept a respectable distance. It felt so uneven, as if they were on a seesaw and she was heaviest because she didn't have the full story, his why-he-was-here. And he knew these things, so he was up in the clouds, enjoying the pink and blue swipes of air.

He waited for her to speak. Hadn't that been their pattern, after all? She'd talk, he'd listen, he'd soothe her, tell her he had her as he held her and lifted her until she was at the top, and still held her as she came down.

"What the fuck, Cue?" And then she wished she could take it back because it sounded so girlfriend-like. And she certainly wasn't his girlfriend. She was Moe's girlfriend, she reminded herself as she tried to shrug off the feeling of Cue's heat, even though he stood a couple of feet away.

"What the fuck, what? What are you asking me, Ayana?"

"Why are you here?"

"As I told you, though you clearly aren't taking me at my word, I'm here to meet a brother. He just showed through, he's in there now, as you can see."

"A hundred thousand places in this city where you could meet a brother," she imitated him, "and you came here. Why?"

"Because I'm going through some heavy shit with my gig."

"What is your gig?"

"Special ops, baby."

"Special ops?" she said, then looked at his face, which he was trying to keep from breaking out in laughter. "So you've got jokes now—"

"Okay, here's the real deal, Ayana. I'm here for a business thing, and I'm here to see you."

"To see me? Why?"

"Because I wanted to see you. Because this thing we've had going for the past four years, as much as I'm into it, and I swear to you I'm into it, is too one-sided. Because right now I could benefit from some reciprocation. I really need somebody holding me up for a few. Somebody I care about, somebody I can trust."

She looked away from his eyes. His eyes gave him an unfair advantage, as she realized in this moment that she'd never seen his eyes in the daylight, never seen that the green had a hint of brown. She could hear him better when she looked away from his eyes. She could hear not just the words but the feeling girding the words.

"My shift is done in two hours," she said. "If you're still here, you can give me a ride home, or wherever."

Nona Dreams

August 2019, Nona's Writing Room, Philadelphia Exurbs

Nona wondered who Miss Dot was really speaking to when she told Lil she was just getting started. Was she really speaking to Nona, transcending the page to address Nona directly, the way her characters sometimes did? And if she was talking to Nona, what exactly was just getting started? The story? Was Lil like that party girl who arrived on the scene and turned the heat up, brought the merriment to people who were otherwise hanging along the wall, engaging in purposeless small talk? Should Nona have opened the book with Lil? "Hell to the no," she said out loud, thinking that Miss Dot should've just kept reading her *Tribune* instead of inserting herself in a conversation that didn't concern her.

Miss Dot reminded Nona of those old-timey women in the neighborhood where she'd grown up who always snickered about her mother behind her back. And after her mother died, and Nona had worked through her grief the way she worked through it, rolling around with man after man after man, the cackling old women turned their judgment on her, labeling her a fast girl, hot in the behind, letting the devil use her, whorish, just downright whorish. Nona forgave them for the names they called her but never ever could for their sanctimony when it came to her mother, who'd always had a dream. A legitimate dream, Nona thought, an upstanding dream. A dream that did not deserve the treatment she'd received as she worked to make her dream come true. Nona felt anger rising at Miss Dot and all the petty shallow-life women like her who were too spineless to summon the courage to dream. Nona stopped herself; getting mad at her characters was never helpful. She was done writing for the day, anyhow.

Bob was in the air again, and Nona was going out with her cousins this evening. She was thinking about what to wear as she unhighlighted the focus button on her computer to allow all the prompts, alerts, texts, emails to stream on in. "How does so much bullshit find its way to my inbox?" she muttered, reminding herself to change the filter for her junk mail to include most of the messages rolling in now. She stopped. There was another reminder about scheduling the MRI to look at the cyst on her pancreas. She didn't need the reminder. She hadn't forgotten, she just hadn't done it. She'd managed not to plague herself over the not-doing. Managed not to give audience to the "Do I have a death wish . . . care so little about myself . . . must be a masochist . . . a martyr" thoughts. Held herself back from envisioning random cells hooking up, replicating, binding, burrowing undetectable in her softness, until the time was both just right and too late. She felt perfectly fine right now, as she decided she'd wear her jagged-edge jeans tonight.

They were going to an old-school soul concert at the Dell in Fairmount Park, and the jeans were tight and showed her big butt and might keep her cousins from haranguing her about her weight loss. She was an only child, and after her parents' relationship devolved, her father had her mother declared unfit and gave Nona to his sister to raise. So her cousins became her sisters, and later her trio of mothers when Nona's mother died. They'd surrounded Nona like a raft of sea lions, crying on her behalf, until the hard grief melted into a softened liquid and she could cry on her own.

The jeans went up easy. Too easy. She stuffed her T-shirt in the jeans to fill them out, then rifled through her closet for something to wear over the tee. Her eye landed on a mint-colored linen jacket like the one that went with the suit Lorna was holding in the scene when the red MINI Cooper crashed through the Marshalls window. She was glad that Lorna managed to get out of the store without paying for the suit. She wished Lorna had handled Ayana differently, though, and accepted that her child had special powers.

This jacket would work; it was coarse, shapeless. She filled the pockets with her keys and phone and wallet to give herself bulk. She looked at herself in the mirror. She gasped. The dancing woman she'd deleted from the Aqua Lounge scene was looking back at her, blankly, still in the loose-fitting brown and red blouse and pinned-up red skirt. Nona turned away. She zigzagged through the bedroom, avoiding the mirror, even as she asked herself what she was afraid of, anyhow. She walked back to the mirror, fists balled as if daring the woman to be there. Saw only herself, her brown-skinned, big-eyed, full-lipped, tiny-waisted, braided-haired self. "You crazy girl," she said to her reflection, then pulled at the jacket to make both it and herself appear wider.

Daylight was just beginning to peel away from the sky as she made her way to the Dell along the Schuylkill Expressway. Most days she hated living so far from the comforting familiarity of her places: her cousin's porch that still caught the buzzing neighborhood gossip; her hair salon where she could get braids, twists, or a press-and-curl with an old-fashioned hot comb; the corner breakfast spot under the El stop where the scrambled cheese eggs were righteous. Her husband, Bob, had grown up in the South, where land was king, and persuaded her out to the exurbs, promising that she would come to covet the openness, the privacy, the new friends she'd meet, new haunts she'd come to love. A decade in and she was still waiting. And it didn't help that the area was so very white, not Center City white, not even suburban Philly white, but a whiteness that felt so entitled and also so threatened, it couldn't fathom coexisting with other than itself.

She turned into the entrance of the Dell and maneuvered her car over the grass toward the young man directing traffic. "Right or left?" she asked.

"I'm sending most people to the left, but pretty ladies like you can take your pick," he said as he smiled a flirty smile that caught the light and showcased his perfect teeth, his heavily lidded eyes.

"I appreciate you." She returned the smile, thinking, You must know I'm old enough to be your momma, right, even as the attention flattered her, and she had to acknowledge the speck of desire that was always going to be there, had to accept it rather than deny or stuff it, lest it come back in a more aberrant form. In another lifetime, she would have asked him where they could meet after the concert was done. She wondered then if a small part of Ayana found it even slightly titillating that the two men with whom she was currently involved were occupying the same space, likely thinking about her, desiring her, as she thought about, desired, them for different reasons. She decided not. Ayana found the whole scenario sordid. Nona thought Ayana to be a much better person than herself.

She turned out of the line of traffic down a narrow lane to an open parking space. The air was busy with the sounds of day and night trading shifts. Lightning bugs choreographed their orange-colored sparks, woodpeckers drilled in the distance, owls tuned their voices, readying for their solos. The earth was soft under her feet as she approached the entrance where her cousins waited. The air smelled of thyme. The moon was trying to show itself against a sky not yet dark as this day streamed its finale of pink and purple and blue assortments. Her cousins looked rapturous under the colors. They'd never abandoned her even in her sunken days. She adored them. She wasn't even affected when the oldest, who'd just turned sixty and was only five years older than Nona, gave off her judgy-mother vibes and said, "Girl, you losing way too much weight."

"Please, big as my butt is," Nona said as she pulled them in a group hug. "And I'm ready to shake this fat ass to some Earth, Wind and Fire wannabe singing 'Boogie Wonderland.'"

She was up on her feet for most of the concert, bobbing and clapping and shaking her shoulders and hips and hollering and singing and laughing to the beat. No one could tell that she was crying, too. She was hitting on something. At first she thought that it was the answer to a question she'd not yet asked. Why was Lil back in Philadelphia? But as the sky darkened, the bass line grew louder, and the drumbeats seemed to tumble from on high, pulsing all inside her body, she realized, yes, it was about Lil, but it was about much more.

Nona had been so focused on Ayana's reaction to Cue being there while Moe was there, and Nona herself wondering what the hell, because she hadn't expected Cue to walk in, either. She was writing so furiously to follow what was happening that she failed to recognize what GG had taught Lil, that the periphery was as important as the main thing. She'd ignored the periphery. Ignored that she was overhearing the back-in-the-day Fifty-Second Street story that Miss Dot had told Moe that turned his face unusually intense. And it had been too easy to push Miss Dot's story out of her conscious mind because then Lil had walked in, Lil shocking Ayana. She'd shocked Nona, too. And with all the big shit happening that she needed to capture, Nona didn't have the time or inclination to capture one of Miss Dot's hundreds of stories.

She'd heard it, though. Not only heard it but internalized every detail, as if sitting right there at that table by the window with Miss Dot and Moe. She'd been intent at the outset of the writing not to allow it on the page. Now that task was even more difficult. She realized that she'd erred by returning to Fifty-Second Street, even though it seemed to slip itself in so naturally, seemed so safe a setting, since it was decades away from when clubs like the Aqua Lounge reigned. She'd have to guard against leaks the way the things important to her sometimes managed to find the smallest crack and drip by drip escape into the narrative. So as the moody drums played on at the Dell, and she laughed and hooted and shook her slimmed-down behind, she also cried.

At the end of the night, she declined her cousins' overtures to stay with one or the other of them instead of taking that long, dark solo ride home. She needed to meet the new day unencumbered, needed the familiarity of her desk overlooking the expanse of wildflowers that her husband had planted in organized rows, even as she'd suggested that he scatter the seeds: Let them do their own thing because they were, after all, wild. She needed to look out that window and reconstruct the scene so that the flowers crossed over their prescribed lines, mixed it up with their soil-mates in unintended ways, rendering the plethora of their shapes and colors all tangled and messy. Were they embracing or were they unintentionally choking the life out of each other? The not knowing frightened her and enthralled her, too.

She despised Miss Dot's stories right now. Even as she could still hear Miss Dot's voice reverberating from deep on the page where she sat by the window in the café telling Lil, telling her, too, you just getting started.

Part Two

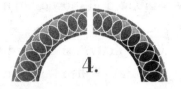

4.

Before the Rainbow

Circa 1790

According to the Mace griots, the family's first Knowing happened in Philadelphia in the late 1700s when eight-year-old Luda saw a rainbow. She sneaked from the backyard of her house, situated on a little block no wider than an alley, populated with Black folk who were prosperous, considering it had been only a decade since the passage of Pennsylvania's Gradual Abolition of Slavery Act. Luda ran to Water Street to hunt for pink stones along the riverbank. She'd dreamed about the stones, which were smooth and flat and shaped like ovals. She saw the rainbow first. It stretched all the way across the river to New Jersey. She understood exactly where New Jersey was because her father worked as an assistant to a cartographer; she and her dad would play map games, and he'd award Luda bits of black licorice when she won. She couldn't wait to tell him about the rainbow and show off to him that she knew where New Jersey was.

"Isn't the rainbow so pretty?" she yelled to the only other person out here, a man most called Ragman Blue, because he spent his days panning for white folks' throwaways.

He tried to ignore Luda, the way he'd tried not to listen when she first spotted him and started chattering away about some stones she'd dreamed about. He didn't like people, especially didn't like people such as her parents and all the others on their block who he thought looked down on him because of the work he did, as if white people favored them because they could draw maps, or fashion shoes for horses, or set a table that had a different fork for every mouthful of food. Given the chance, he'd tell them they still were not favored, never would be favored, and wait just a minute and Old Charlie would have them right back in chains.

"I sees nuttin."

"Nothing," Luda said, correcting him because her father maintained that it was better to teach those who didn't know than to ridicule them.

"Like I says, I see *nuttin*," he said, emphasizing his pronunciation. "Further, gal, would you let me be. You breaking up my peering. Folk think this easy, but it takes concentration to speck worthiness out here."

"Oh, I understand. I just didn't want you to miss the rainbow," she said, looking back up at the sky. She gasped then because the rainbow appeared to be twisting itself into a knot and wringing itself out the way her mother squeezed excess water from muslin sheets before hanging them to dry. Instead of streams of water, though, the rainbow dripped its colors into the river, and the river lapped them up. And now there was an arc of blankness, of colorless nothingness, in the sky where the rainbow had been.

"Uh, uh, uh," she exclaimed, "you must see that. Please tell me that you do." She pointed to the sky where the rainbow had been. "And now they're people, oh no, so many people sick, turning gray. I think they might be dead. You see them, too? Please tell me that you see them, too."

Her tone was so frantic that he stopped what he was doing and looked at the sky. Normal as ever to him, its early-morning pinkness mixing with tatters of soft white. He picked up his knapsack and walked slowly to where Luda stood, her eyes fixed on the sky, her mouth open, staring trancelike. He pushed beyond his disdain for Luda's people and all the other Black Philadelphians like them, which allowed him to mellow the tone of his voice from its usual gruffness. "Gimme your hand, Luda girl," he whispered. "I'mma walk you on home, 'cause you done gone crazy in the head. A danger to be out here like this alone."

He curled his hand around hers as softly as he could, conscious of his calloused fingers, even as he reasoned that she wasn't feeling much of anything now. She walked stiffly like a toy wooden soldier being led by a string. He picked her up so she wouldn't step in a mound of straw-covered horse droppings, then carried her the rest of the way. She was deadweight heavy in his arms. He yelled as he turned up her block, "Ruth,

Ruth, your chile needs seeing to right this instant, plus she heavy."

A voice came from an open window across the street. "Ruth just ran around the corner looking for Luda. Luda, where you been, child? Your mother practically hysterical you weren't in the backyard where she left you."

Blue talked back to the fancy dotted Swiss curtain drifting in and out of the window. "Luda gone sick in the head. Like she don't see or hear nuttin this instant."

"Bring her over here, Ragman, and then you run around the corner and find Ruth."

"No, you run 'round the corner and find Ruth. I'm tired," he said. "I'll sit with Luda."

"I have to get myself presentable first. And what are you tired from except picking through the trash?"

"What you tired from 'cept being ugly?" He listened to her window slam shut as he situated his knapsack on the step to make a pillow for Luda to sit upon. He set her down, then sat next to her and took it as a good sign when she sighed and leaned her head against his arm.

Now he watched the woman across the street emerge from her house, parasol in tow. "Thought you was getting presentable." He laughed, sarcasm dripping.

"My religion won't allow me to say what you need to hear," she huffed as she ran toward them. "Luda, baby, you in distress?" She put her hand around the child's chin and lifted her face.

"She need her momma. Go fetch her now." He relished the

opportunity to bark demands in the same way people were always telling him what to do: white folk, his own folk.

He listened to her footsteps hurrying against the cobblestones. Then he turned his attention back to Luda. "You know where you be?" he asked, using his softened tone again. He felt her nodding against his arm. "You still seeing messes in the sky t'aint there?"

"It was there," she said. "It was there. It was, it was."

"Okay, maybe you seen it. Maybe you sees what I can't," he said, not wanting to agitate her further. But also unpeeling himself to the notion that perhaps she was a bit of a seer. "Sound like a scary sumpin for a little gal to see. A bunch of dead folk."

She nodded against his arm.

"Was they mostly white folk?"

"At first," she said haltingly.

"And den?"

"Then they looked like us. Just falling down dead."

He could hear trembling in her voice, so he told her she didn't have to talk about it if it was scaring her.

"I'm not so afraid with you sitting here," she said. "Thank you, Mr. Blue."

He wasn't sure whether he wanted to laugh or cry. Such unfamiliar words for him to hear, a "thank-you" and a "mister" in front of his name that did not include the down-putting Ragman. "Hmph," he said finally. "I'mma just sit here, den, so you don't have to be scared. And if it help you to tell me again what you saw, I'm not only hearin, I'm believing, too, in what you done seen, yeah. You done seen a Knowin'."

According to the story passed down through generations of Maces, Luda's vision foretold the yellow fever epidemic that practically turned the bustling city of Philadelphia, the birthplace of the nascent democracy, into a pile of smoldering rags. Black people were pressed into service to care for the sick and wrap the bodies of the dead because of the unfounded notion that they were immune to the disease. Blue tried to warn them that they were not immune. He knew this, he insisted, because he'd heard Luda describe what she'd seen the day the rainbow fell, the bodies that first were all white before moving on to Black.

Blue earned his way into the story of Luda: for taking such care of her that morning, for believing in her gift of clairvoyance, and for giving the clairvoyance its name—the Knowing.

And after Luda's death, her name became sacred to the Mace women who followed her path. They uttered her name only among one another, and even then it was in whispered reverence, or in prayer, or right before a Knowing ritual when they said aloud their vows, one vow affirming that Luda's name should never pass their lips outside the community of Mace women.

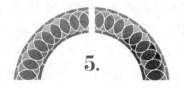

5.
After the Rainbow

Now, Luda's people respected her eccentricities. Only soft fabrics against her skin, velvet or silk, no muslin. Her thick hair stretched wide and high in massive tangles because she couldn't tolerate the comb moving across her scalp. She might have been avoided like a Medusa figure, but her face was rapturous. Beyond the parenthesis-shaped cleft in her chin, the full mouth, the politely slanted nose, there was the major attraction, her eyes. Dark like carbon, generously sized, thickly lashed, brows so perfectly shaped they appeared to have been painted on. Most of her descendants inherited the eyes. Even Ayana had them. Their eyes were difficult to turn away from, especially, it seemed, for polite men seeking to do a woman's bidding.

The Mace women, though, were oblivious to the way certain men reacted to their eyes. They attributed their knack for attracting their husbands—who were hardworking loyalists, always poised to indulge their wives' inclinations—as God's way of ensuring that they could use their gift of prophecy. And the husbands did indulge them: indulged their wives' claim to a sacred clairvoyance, indulged their ritual time, even indulged their want to keep their own name.

The practice was passed down from Luda. The man she would marry had no last name. He was known only as Buck. So she proclaimed that he would be Buck Mace. And though future husbands of Mace women certainly had last names that they held on to, the Mace women followed Luda's example and retained Mace as theirs.

The husbands suffered a measure of alienation that the strangeness of their wives sometimes caused, especially through the generations at the barbershop when they were accused of making normal men look bad. But they were not swayed. Unrelated by DNA though the Mace husbands were, it was as if they'd all inherited an absolute-devotion-to-my-lady gene.

In the 1920s such a man built the house still occupied by the Maces in Southwest Philly, upwind from the river behind the railroad tracks, once lush with overgrowth and mosquitoes and migrating birds and migrating people. The house was originally hidden from view by the woods, until the woods became concrete with waterlines and gas lines below, electric poles above, and houses, so many houses springing up like mushrooms from none to hundreds overnight.

The Mace house sat in the middle of the line of row houses on either side, a substantial oak tree out front planted by GG's father. The tree housed hummingbirds in the summer, and the family spread feeders all around the house because they believed the hummingbirds communicated with the ancestors, and if one flew in front of them and sat there staring, wings moving constantly, even while appearing to be still, it meant that all would be well.

The house was distinct because it was not a standard row. Because it was there first, and had claimed its own perimeter, its space in the front and back and on the sides, it was disconnected from the other houses, as the Maces would be disconnected from the people occupying the smaller rows, with the smaller porches, with the smaller people with low tolerance for oddness. And even though the house was set back from the street, farther back than the neighbors', in the spring and summer, the Maces' chanting sifted through their open windows. And after autumn claimed the leaves of the oak, it was easy to see them gathering at dawn and sunset, easy to view their swan moves, their jumping and shaking. The food aromas were present in every season, so many food aromas. And the Maces would have been happy to share. But their generosity was rebuffed, sometimes so haughtily that they were confused, not upset, though. Their calling was their calling, and that, not the approval of their neighbors, was the important thing.

The interior of the house was spectacularly constructed. The chair rails and crown moldings had been carved by hand. The floorboards were wide planks of oak and maple and pine, laid like sunbeams connecting to the circle where their rituals took place. The centerpiece of the living room was the ceiling where a rainbow formed by stained glass made up the skylight and dazzled the space below when the sunrise glowed through as it did the morning GG and her granddaughter Lil met the baker's wife.

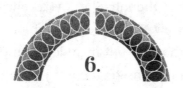

6.

The Baker's Wife

Philadelphia 1977

The sun was preparing to squeeze through the cracks in the darkness as young Lil tiptoed through the living room to meet GG on the enclosed porch in the grand three-story house she shared with her parents; her older sister, Bev; her baby brother, Miles; her grandmother GG; and their affable pet pig named Pig, whose oinks sounded like human laughter.

Lil was set to take notes for GG while GG interviewed a prospective seeker. GG always enlisted either Bev or Lil as a scribe when she conducted business so that she could study a person's affect. And she always scheduled the intake sessions for daybreak because she believed the transition between dark and light opened places in the mind and the heart that were otherwise shuttered.

This used to be such a favorite undertaking for Lil, she didn't even mind getting up before the sun.

She minded now, though. She was a college senior with an expanding worldview. She'd get dizzy when she considered future possibilities that did not include singing and dancing at dawn and sometimes sunset; preparing for the rituals, the after-feasts; sitting in on meetings to understand GG's reasoning for accepting or rejecting a seeker's case, learning how to negotiate the way GG did, memorizing the stories handed down from the ancestors, the chants, the verses. Part of Lil still wanted to do all those things. She idolized her grandmother. She just wished that GG had not skipped over Lil's mother, Hortense, and sister, Bev, to stand Lil on a too-high pedestal to prepare her to serve when GG no longer could, as the keeper of the culture, the bearer of traditions, the family's leader ensuring that generations of Mace women to come would practice the gift of prophecy as the ancestors had.

The enclosed porch looked out on their mammoth oak, whose roots had begun to spread below the foundation. Sometimes in the stillness, they could almost sense the roots' movement, stretching farther under the basement floor, baby shoots curious about what was above them, pulling away from the main roots, trying to push up, to break through to the other side.

The woman sitting across from GG at the round glass-covered wicker table folded and unfolded her hands in quick succession. GG gave her a ball and told her to squeeze it a few times. "It might help you relax, and whenever you're ready, you can say whatever you need to say about what prompted you to seek us out."

The woman squeezed the ball and told GG about Mr. Baker,

her husband, who, true to his name, ran a thriving West Philly bakery that he'd inherited from his father, who'd gotten a bargain-basement deal during the white flight of the 1950s. Her husband was a solid man, "a steady Eddie, if you know what I mean," she said, and then listed his doings, which included church deacon, Boy Scout troop leader, committeeman for the city's Democratic Party. She paused, caressed the ball, and said that he was also a bit of a flirt. She described how he turned his conversations with the women customers into some kind of foreplay as he gently assembled the twisted glazed doughnuts in square white boxes lined with waxed paper, then tied and triple-bowed the boxes with twine, calling on his husky voice, his sexy voice, to say some variation of "The sugar I flaked onto the hot dough lightly fried in butter is not nearly as sweet as the curve of your lips when you smile." Or, when slicing a substantial piece of chocolate layer cake to wrap and bag, he'd exclaim, "What a brown beauty for such a brown beauty as you." Sometimes, she said, he'd just look at a woman as he gave her change for her purchase and shake his head slowly and say, "My, my, my," as if he were a preacher talking about the goodness of God.

"Was that hard for you to watch and hear?" GG asked.

Mrs. Baker rolled the ball back and forth across the table as if she herself were kneading dough. "I did not discourage it," she said. "He was, you know, he was touching places in a woman that burned to feel desirable. And even though our baked goods are freshly handmade, you know, our pricing can't compete with Acme. So absent his—his fresh talking, many of the women would just go someplace cheaper unless they needed a special birthday cake or something."

"So it was good for business."

"It was, it was very good," Mrs. Baker said. Describing how she came downstairs into the store from their living quarters around three in the afternoon mainly to help ring up the schoolkids crowding in for brownies and doughnut holes, she said, "And that's the time of day he went missing."

"Tell me about that," GG said in a whisper.

"He was gone, just gone. I stepped into the store as always, the sun blazing, the store was filled with kids jostling to get the best view into the glass-covered shelves, smudges and thumbprints everywhere on the glass even though we had signs all over the place begging people not to press against the counters. I called for him, then I yelled for him. The kids were so loud, I could barely hear my own voice. Then one little girl with dirty glasses and unevenly parted braids pushed through the short wooden gate that closed off access to the workers' side of the counter, and she tugged my shirt, it was my favorite light blue shirt, I had just sprayed it with starch and ironed it, and it was so stiff that at first I didn't feel her tugging it. And when I did and looked down at her, the first thing I saw were her glasses. They were so dirty. And I wondered, How can I be thinking about this child's glasses when I can't figure out where my husband is." She paused and swallowed then and sat back against the chair's thick white cushions and looked out the window at the massive oak tree as if searching for her husband even among the branches.

Family Spirit

GG filled the silence by reassuring her that it was normal to notice unrelated details in times of distress. "It is the mind trying to help us, to redirect us from our terror," she said as she motioned to Lil, who poured tea into a porcelain cup and set it along with a petite sugar bowl in front of Mrs. Baker. Mrs. Baker spooned sugar in the cup and stirred the tea continuously as she told how the little girl said that Mr. Baker had gone for a walk.

"I said, 'A walk?' And I ran out the store and looked up and down the street. The child followed me outside, and I asked her, 'Did he tell you he was going for a walk? What exactly did he say?' I was yelling at her, I felt bad for yelling at her, it wasn't her fault, and then out of the blue I asked her how she could possibly even see out of those glasses. I took the glasses from her face and fogged them with my breath and pulled a hankie from my apron pocket and rubbed them, and I had to do that about three times because the lenses had accumulated a week's worth of dust and grime. And I kept asking her what exactly Mr. Baker had said. And she kept repeating the same thing, that he'd said he was done and was gonna take a long walk to nowhere. What does that even mean?" Her voice shook, and she stopped talking and picked up the ball and began squeezing it furiously.

"A long walk to nowhere," GG repeated. "And you believe the child?"

"Why would she lie, and besides my reasoning is that someone who was so busy observing things that she didn't know her own glasses were filthy must have an otherwise heightened awareness about what was going on around her beyond what she could see with her physical eyes."

"I cannot disagree with that," GG said as Mrs. Baker sipped her tea.

Lil used the silence to stretch her fingers and massage her wrist as she imagined how she would have reacted to Mrs. Baker's situation. Not the disappearance but the husband's flirtations. She understood the business reality of his risqué talk, and if she'd walked in Mrs. Baker's shoes, she would have allowed it, even encouraged it. But unlike Mace women from previous generations, Lil did have a sense of the effect her eyes had on a man, also how her hips drew attention, the fullness of her mouth, the tilt of her head. She would have embraced the challenge of having a husband with a wandering eye. Would have found it thrilling to entice his eyes back to her at the end of the day. She didn't want a man's devotion to her to be a given the way it seemed to be a given for her mother, her grandmother, her married aunts and cousins. Let the good Lord mete out the unmerited favor, the grace, that she devoutly received. But when it came to human men, she wanted to work for it; she craved the excitement of the hunt, the chase, the titillation of not knowing for sure if she'd prevail, and then, only after she'd earned it, reveling in the sound of his "Damn, baby, damn" moans moving through her. She didn't envision herself ever marrying if it meant eliminating that kind of excitement.

Mrs. Baker had finished her tea, and Lil picked up her pen as GG asked about the police's involvement.

Mrs. Baker huffed and said the no-count detective did

everything except say directly that her husband had run off with another woman. "I gave them names of everyone, his deacon friends, and neighborhood friends, and frequent customers he stayed in touch with, his family, I gave them a list of at least fifty people. And I contacted them all. Every last one. Not the police. Me. I did it. I've kept the business going by myself, too. Me. By myself." She banged the ball on the table, and it rolled toward GG.

GG cupped her hands gently over the ball and asked what made her so certain that her husband had not run off with another woman.

"You have had a husband, correct?" Mrs. Baker more declared than asked. GG didn't respond other than to fix her eyes on Mrs. Baker in what Bev and Lil joked was her gangster stare.

Mrs. Baker lowered her head then as if she were about to pray. "I feel it in my heart," she said, "that's how I am so certain."

"Do you feel that he is alive?" GG asked.

"I do, but I need to know for sure." Mrs. Baker rushed her words—"I just need to know if he is alive, and where he is, and if he is not, then how, I just—"

"I have a sense of what you need, Mrs. Baker," GG said. "But you should know that we make no guarantees about what we will come to know. And certainly, if it all remains a blank slate, we return your fee in full."

Mrs. Baker sat up straighter. A sense of hope, of relief, softened her eyes, slackened her jaws. But when GG quoted the fee, she watched Mrs. Baker's face collapse.

"Ah," she said, "ah, I can't, we just took out a new mortgage, for new ovens, we just—I did not expect the fee—Oh, dear God."

GG's expression didn't change. By now she was accustomed to such a reaction. It opened the door for her to transact on behalf of the Mace family's needs in other than direct cash payments. It was how she'd garnered the run of Ridley Creek State Park every Sunday morning for Pig before the regular staff arrived because they'd helped the live-in groundskeeper course-correct his life. Similarly, they hadn't paid a fee for oil changes or brake pads or a new battery or alternator in the last year. And every Saturday evening, a healthy round of fresh-cut Delmonico rib eye was left on the inlet that led to the porch. Her most meaningful transaction though, was when they helped the pastor of their church foil a move to oust him. He paid them in a way impossible to quantify, by respecting their right to believe that God had gifted them with a special gene, and it was not heresy for the Maces to proclaim it. When he saw them parade into the church in their elaborate handsewn garb with their freestanding hair, strutting like royalty, he'd change whatever his message was to be and preach instead about the spiritual gift of prophecy. And though most still considered them witches or sorcerers and avoided them, feared them, the Maces at least had seats in the congregation and felt welcomed by the pastor sitting high on the altar.

"I'm willing to accept other forms of payment," GG said. "You can redeem our expertise in exchange for your own."

"For what? For baked goods?"

Family Spirit

"Yes, for baked goods." GG went on to detail the large family gatherings that could benefit from her breakfast casserole and bread pudding, twice monthly first thing in the morning, and otherwise smaller amounts of rolls and Danish and such during the week for the next three months. "I can cut the fee by an appreciable amount, and you can take three months to pay the cash portion as well."

Lil made sure to capture these details. They would be included in the contract that Mrs. Baker would sign. They would also frustrate the family line of GG's youngest sister, Helene. Helene's daughters and especially her granddaughters had begun to show their discontent at GG's inclination to take on what they called charity cases. Sometimes during family meetings, they'd release a barely perceptible sound of teeth being sucked, huffs of breath pulled back, fingers curling into fists. They'd complain to Bev and Lil about all the dollar bills the family was leaving on the table. Bev and Lil turned a deaf ear. If a family storm over finances was brewing, Bev and Lil would rise or fall with GG. Anyhow, Lil did the math in her head as she took notes. She knew the cost of a half-size cup of the Bakers' bread pudding, so a pan large enough to satisfy a dozen people for their post-ritual feasts, in addition to their breakfast casserole loaded with eggs and cheese and sausage, not to mention the buttery yeast rolls, was a favorable deal for the Maces and would also enable Mrs. Baker to access their services.

After GG and Mrs. Baker came to terms, Lil and GG sat on the porch and sipped more tea, and GG asked Lil what did she think. Lil looked over her notes and said that she was struck by money being an issue; perhaps Mr. Baker was a gambler or otherwise in hock to the Mob and they made him disappear. Though that hadn't been Lil's first thought. She didn't say her first thought, that Mr. Baker likely loved his life, devoted to his craft and his wife, but he yearned for more. And his yearning became too large for him to ignore. Lil feared her grandmother may have sensed that Lil was talking about herself, not Mr. Baker. So Lil didn't verbalize that thought.

"Certainly a possibility," GG said, "but the child tips the scale in the other direction."

"Oh my God, does she ever," Lil exclaimed. "Who wouldn't believe that little girl. With those pitifully dirty glasses."

"Likely," GG said, "Mr. Baker was overwhelmed by his responsibility, not because he couldn't do it but because he didn't want to."

"Very likely." Lil agreed.

They sat quietly, watching the brilliantly colored hummingbirds fly to the feeder hanging outside the porch. Their motion so constant, even when they were still.

7.

Saturday-Morning Rituals

Two days later, Lil rubbed her skin with jojoba oil and carefully stepped into the elaborate ritual garment that had been hand-stitched by GG and GG's sisters and included pieces of velvet, organza, silk, and cotton from the clothes of dead family members. GG had pointed out a pearl button at the top of the dress when she'd presented it to Lil and told her that the pearl had belonged to Luda. Lil knew the story of their Mother Ancestor; it had been her favorite growing up. She held her breath, hoping GG wouldn't recount Luda's prophecy when the rainbow spilled its color from the sky. She was relieved when GG did not; hearing it would sadden Lil, because it would remind her that she'd outgrown the story, and that would spiral into her ruminating about other things in her life that she was outgrowing.

She flapped the top of the dress in so the pearl didn't show. She fingered the more meaningful breast pocket cut from her grandfather's handkerchief, white with red embroidery. She thought the scent of his Old Spice aftershave still clung to the handkerchief. He'd been gone for a half a year, and she missed his soft eyes, which had always made her feel as if she were the best little girl God ever created. She never felt the weight of expectations from him, could even complain to him about how the early-Saturday-morning rituals kept her from a Friday-night basement house party where she could sweat her hair out to the beat and, after, devour pancakes and cheese eggs at midnight with her two besties, who lived on her block, and whom she'd known since toddlerhood, and who weren't put off by her family's weirdness. "Just take the rituals one at a time, Lillianna," her grandfather would say. "They'll always be another party, and you can manage anything one at a time."

But she no longer had him to remind her. No longer could she confess to him that she felt like running away rather than fulfilling the role GG was prepping her for. "What do I do when I look at my future and feel like I'm suffocating?" she'd ask him.

"Well, first, breathe, Lillianna," he'd say. "You can't do anything if you don't first allow yourself to breathe."

"Why didn't you keep breathing, then, Grandpop?" she said now, as she pulled the dress off and stomped on it. "You knew how much I needed you." She picked up the dress and held it to it her and rubbed the pocket against her cheek and cried.

She re-dressed and hurried downstairs and, with Pig at her feet, received her extended family, who arrived in twos and threes, her grandmother's sisters, her aunts and cousins—some lovable, some loathsome, some who Lil thought were downright sinister, like her cousin Carlotta, Helene's granddaughter.

Lil and Carlotta had been born a week apart, and Helene complained that GG hoarded all the attention for Lil, leaving none for her grand. As the girls grew, so did Helene's propensity for singling out everything GG did that she thought favored Lil over Carlotta, even protesting when GG provided cakes for their joint sixth birthday party, because Lil's cake had three flowers and Carlotta's just one. Lil, trying to broker peace, whispered to Carlotta that they could just cut out the names and trade cakes because the extra flower meant nothing to her. "Keep your stinking cake," Carlotta hissed under her breath, "and be glad my grandmother doesn't throw it in GG's face." And though GG and Helene managed to do a tango over the years, holding each other at bay one minute, twirling with sisterly affection into each other's arms the next, there was no closeness between Lil and Carlotta. Not for lack of effort from Lil, who was skilled at reading people and knew what to do to win them over; Carlotta was a tough yam to candy, though.

"Hey, cuz, how you be?" Lil said now, as Carlotta walked onto the enclosed porch and stepped out of her shoes and lined them up next to the others.

"A lot better if I didn't have to get up before the sun," she said, shaking her arms from her sweater and putting it on the rack.

"I hear you," Lil said, fingering the top of her dress to make sure Luda's pearl was out of view. She wondered now about GG's motivation for adding the pearl. Was it just to provoke

Helene and, by extension, Carlotta? "And I'm loving your hair," Lil added.

"I just hit it with a warm comb, you could do the same with yours," Carlotta said. She looked at Lil's hair and grimaced.

"A warm comb and some magic," Lil said.

"Definitely some magic," Carlotta said as she moved toward the door that led into the living room. Then stepped back so Bev could come through. Bev said a curt "Morning," Carlotta responding in kind.

"Why you always bending over to be nice to her?" Bev said to Lil once Carlotta was out of earshot.

"I don't know. I guess I just feel bad for her that she thinks she's always being shortchanged."

"That's her shit, not yours," Bev said. "And GG wants you to light the candles."

"See, that's what I'm talking 'bout. Why can't Carlotta ever light the candles?"

"Who are you, her booking agent? You know like I know, you'll carry your butt on in there and do your diligence."

✦ ✦ ✦

Lil put a match to the candles as they all formed a circle over the sacred space in the living room centered under the stained-glass skylight of Luda's rainbow. GG passed around a linen napkin that belonged to Mr. Baker and read the details from Lil's notes. Then she led them in a prayer of purification passed down from the ancestors, meant to free them of judgment and nonbelief as they opened themselves to the birth of a Knowing.

Family Spirit

When GG was finished, she raised her arms as if conducting an orchestra. Lil loved her grandmother's arms; they were both soft and strong, and all was well with the world when Lil sank into them.

The air in the room was still. The only movement came from the tinkling of the chandelier's crystal drops; the only sound came from the vibrant colors of their ritual garb, shouting.

Helene began to sing. Her extended vibrato encircled them, causing one or several to join her in the wordless song. They danced then, moving their arms like swans; the young twirled on their toes, the old thumped flat-footed to and fro. GG began to chant in rhythmic pulses of known words like "vanished," "gone," "tell us," mixed with indecipherable syllables strung together like a necklace that mesmerized because no one stone resembled the other.

Lil turned around and around, her hands stretching toward Luda's rainbow, her back arched as she concentrated on Mr. Baker. At times like this, as she listened to her grandmother's lovely chants and danced to the syncopated beat formed by the footsteps that were flitting and pounding, she'd feel so fused to her family, so enamored by them, so connected even with the irritants and complainers and conspirers. The astounding sense of unity allowed her to drift like a wavy line that could enter otherwise inaccessible spaces and then return to the swaying and dancing and melodies. But today, as she surrendered to the drifting sensation, she saw herself with a man in a colorless room. They were wrapped in a smoky haze and feeding each other melting chocolate bars. Lil was laughing.

She was happy. She tried to unsee the man, his eyes shining with curiosity when he took in her presence, his self-assured smile, his employee badge that stuck to his sweaty skin as he pressed against her. She kept her eyes closed, didn't dare look up at her grandmother, who was likely waiting for her to take to the center of the circle as a Knowing related to the Bakers inhabited her. This thing Lil was coming to know had nothing to do with the Bakers. It was seamy, as she felt the man's breaths pushing in her ear, heard his heartbeats throbbing like African drummers calling on the harvest; his sheets were hot beneath her back. She couldn't believe this was what she was seeing in this moment of all moments. She prayed for the Knowing spirit not to pull her into the center of the circle, where she would no longer be able to act under her own power, where she would commence to babble and cry and reveal the foretelling she was experiencing. How such a revelation would not only disappoint but also mortify her grandmother; how it would delight her cousins, anxious as they were to knock her from the pedestal where GG had placed her, where Lil never ever wanted to be. She could already hear their whispered laughter: *Daaamn, she supposed to be GG's handpicked all that, and her Knowing is about her fucking some dude still wearing his work ID.*

She focused on the ceiling, on Luda's rainbow, prayed that the ancestors might spare a bit of compassion for her right now. Right now, please, Spirit of Mother Ancestor Luda, right now, she prayed.

And then it happened: Her cousin Carlotta began to jump up and down, spinning as she did, then moaning as the others encircled her, encouraging her. They took turns touching and agreeing, putting their hands on Carlotta's shoulders as she twitched and cried out.

GG began chanting, "Speak, daughter of Mother Ancestor, speak." And the others joined in the chant as they passed Carlotta around the circle, each giving her an embrace, whispering encouragement in her ear. When it was Lil's turn, she reached out for Carlotta, but Carlotta stiffened, backed up, shook her head, then let out a guttural howl like a woman giving birth as the others moved in closer. She began to speak then. Her words fell in incoherent jumbles at first. And then broken sentences.

"Slimy, so slimy," she gasped. And Lil was paralyzed, thinking that Carlotta had absorbed the same foretelling as Lil. That had happened only once in the years since Lil had been allowed to join the rituals. She fought the urge to cover Carlotta's mouth. But GG was already encouraging her.

"What is slimy?" GG asked in the gentlest whispers.

"The bloodworms. Ugh, the bloodworms," Carlotta said as she jerked and pulled at her dress as if bloodworms were crawling on her, though Lil was able to breathe again because Carlotta was not describing her as slimy.

"Where are the bloodworms, child?"

"They are hanging for the shad to eat, and the perch, and the trout."

"And who eats the fish? Does Mr. Baker eat the fish?"

"He is in a box?"

"Is it a coffin?"

"He sits in the box." Carlotta sat on the floor cross-legged then.

"What does he do in the box?"

"He cooks fish over a Sterno flame."

"Where is the box, where is he?"

"Under the overpass of the expressway, then to the river to fish. He likes it."

"What does he like?"

"The box, the fish, he is free?"

"For all time?" GG asked on a whisper.

"His wife will talk him into returning home when it snows. But for now he likes it here." Carlotta began to cry. She shook uncontrollably, not uncommon for those the Knowing spirit hit as the physical body worked to regain its center, its balance, its homeostasis, after being inhabited by such an uncommon object as a future landscape; the body was not privy to what the heart and soul accepted, that this visionary nugget was not invasive. And since it did not understand that this was a gift, the body did what it was designed to do to defend itself: It shook and went hot and cold; it sped up the heart, the breath, lent a hyperacuity to all the senses so that the receptors from touch to sight, sound, and smell, even taste were magnified. It was an overreaction, like a cytokine storm; it could feel torturous to a body experiencing tomorrow today.

GG hit the triangle three times, and the cousins helped Carlotta to stand and wrapped a blanket around her and led her to the high-backed chair. They helped her sip black tea, and when GG hit the triangle again, they commenced to sing the tune that they believed had the power to return the body to itself, to its calm.

Family Spirit

Pour back into us your peace that we let go, the gift,
  the glorious gift,
calm us with your glow, from head to heart to soul,
  to make us whole,
that we may know. The gift, the glorious gift.
Oh, sweet, sweet Spirit, calm us with your glow,
that we may know. That we may know.

Carlotta began to settle down. Her grandmother sat next to her and held her hand. The others surrounded Carlotta and whispered their congratulations, as if she'd just delivered a glistening, slippery newborn, a foretelling, an otherwise unknowable thing.

Lil held back. Pig had sidled up to her and was squealing in discomfort. Lil stroked Pig. "You're okay, and so am I," she whispered. "Okay, maybe I'm not at the moment, but I will be." She nudged Pig to walk with her toward the back of the house. She opened the door and Pig pranced outside. Lil stood on the steps and watched Pig run through the yard, pausing between laps to roll around on the dew-tipped grass. She thought about Mr. Baker as she listened to Pig's happy squeals, glad for the space out here, feeling somewhat free. She thought about herself, too.

Lil decided to skip the post-ritual feast today. She hated to abandon Bev, but she had papers due Monday and needed to spend concentrated time at the library. At least she convinced herself that was the reason, knowing really that her extended family was exhausting. She changed into jeans and a sweatshirt and parked her book bag at the breakfast room door and peeled back the variegated air into the breakfast room.

There were her grandmother GG and GG's sisters, Flora, the middle child, and Helene, the youngest. The sisters had four daughters and two sons between them, four granddaughters, and two grandsons.

The men and boys, save Miles, who was too young, dipped in and out of the breakfast room to heap their plates. Since only the women had the gift of Knowing, the men were not privy to their rituals or their pre- and post-activities. That suited them, as they grabbed food and disappeared into whatever man-space they'd designated. They'd smoke cigars and talk politics and Eagles; they bragged or ruminated about their present or past trials and triumphs with women. They traded jokes and sips of whiskey and tidbits from the older to the younger about being a man, what made a man, and from the younger to the older about how to tie their high-tops and shape their hair.

It was barbershop talk, where anything went, any joke was okay, any argument was received and returned in order.

Lil sensed that the Mace women were living easy at the moment, too. They were in that remarkable between time when the Spirit still lingered, when they rested their resentments and envies and rivalries. They were glowing, warmhearted, agreeable. It was magic. Lil thought about delaying her date with the library as she watched Miles in the middle of the floor,

Family Spirit

clapping when he rolled his Tonka truck toward Pig and Pig nosed it back to Miles. But she knew it would be short-lived, it always was.

"Headed to the library, Mommy," she said. She picked up Miles and squeezed him and juggled him in her arms and approached her mother, who was piling generous helpings of Mrs. Baker's breakfast casserole on the plates. Bev poured coffee from the percolator into mugs that, according to family lore, had been formed and baked by GG's mother.

"You're not going to eat?" her mother asked as she tilted her cheek so that Lil could kiss her.

"I filled up on tasting as I unwrapped the trays. And I'd love to sit with y'all, but I've got to play catch-up with these papers I need to write," she said.

"Your notes on Mrs. Baker were incredibly detailed," Bev said. "I can imagine how that bit into your time."

Lil nodded and turned toward the expansive oval table. But before she could say her goodbyes, GG's sister Helene cleared her throat and said that she had something to say. She always had something to say. The air over the table tightened. GG pursed her lips in the most subtle way. Flora, always feeling pressured to take sides, folded her hands softly as if she were about to pray. Lil braced herself as she looked down at the new vinyl floor her father had just installed before he hit the road for his latest work detail. Portland this time. He'd be gone for three weeks. Lil missed him, but she hardly blamed him as she looked at the assemblage around the table. Not that they weren't pleasant to look at—they were pretty people, with their wide gushy smiles and Luda's dark oversize eyes, their wonderfully wild crinkly hair, their bronzed-honey skin coloring that naturally rouged their cheekbones. Lil was happy to have inherited their looks. It was their critical, backbiting ways that made them difficult to be around. Especially Helene, and her daughters, and her granddaughter Carlotta.

Lil squeezed Miles again and smooched his forehead to fortify herself against whatever Helene had to say. She put Miles back down to continue his play with Pig and the Tonka truck. She loved Miles in a way that was pure and weightless, unencumbered by expectations.

"I would just like to know," Helene said as she sipped her coffee, "who decided that Lil should be the first to wear Mother Ancestor's pearl."

"Lil was wearing her pearl?" Carlotta blurted, then sat back quickly, aware that she'd spoken out of turn.

"Yes, she was, and I decided," GG said calmly. GG was mostly calm when Helene confronted her. She was older and had rank on her side.

"And what gives you the right? You could have consulted me."

GG put a forkful of the breakfast casserole in her mouth. She took her time chewing, closing her eyes as she did. "Heavenly, just heavenly," she said after she'd swallowed. "That was a good negotiation with Mrs. Baker, don't you think, Lil? We'll enjoy these after each ritual for the next three months."

"Really? That's wonderful," said conflict-averse Flora, rushing to move on from the Luda pearl controversy.

Family Spirit

"Plenty of sweets for you guys to pack up and take home, too," Bev said. "The lemon-filled doughnuts are to die for." She spooned up a plate of casserole for her mother and told her to have a seat, she would finish up.

"I'll help," Lil rushed to say, feeling her guilt mount about abandoning Bev.

"No, you won't, don't you have papers to write?" Bev said.

"Don't deny her the opportunity. That's the least she could do after having the honor of wearing Mother Ancestor's pearl," Helene countered.

"Back to the pearl," Bev tried to say under her breath, but everybody heard. Carlotta even gasped. "Sorry, no disrespect, Aunt Helene," Bev said.

"Yes, back to the pearl," Helene sniped. "GG, you don't get to decide that a thing so coveted in this family goes to your granddaughter alone."

"I did decide, Helene." GG stood as she spoke. "And what of it, Helene?"

"Nothing of it, please," Flora shouted. "You guys, really. Can't we set a better example about sisterly love for our young people?"

"My sister and I have plenty of it, we're willing to share it," Bev said as she winked at Lil.

"I'm not having much more of your sass today, Bev," Helene said. "Hortense, you dropped the ball with teaching this one respect for her elders."

Bev gasped, and Hortense turned toward Helene and glared, and Carlotta said under her breath, "You right about that, Grandmom."

Lil's heart beat double-time as she watched Bev put down the spoon she was holding and fix her eyes on Carlotta. Bev was a fighter. She was tall and slim and had once taken down a man twice her size who'd erupted at GG when she refunded his money, their protocol when they couldn't forecast a seeker's future. He'd gotten in GG's face and demanded that they try again. Bev, always by her grandmother's side during such transactions, asked him politely to leave. He turned to her, panting, enraged, as if he were going to attack her. He never had a chance. Bev delivered a body blow first, and then a knee, and he crumbled, howling, until he could pick himself up and limp away.

"Sorry, cuz," Bev said to Carlotta, "but you don't get to insult my mother to my face."

Lil was at the counter then, taking the spoon from Bev's hand, pulling her away, saying that she needed her help with something in the basement. "Important, Bev, please," she begged.

"Bev, see what your sister needs," GG said. "This is not your fight."

"It's nobody's fight." Flora pushed her voice into the tangled air as Lil and Bev left the kitchen to the sound of more voices raised, but at least Bev wouldn't be involved, Lil thought.

The air in the basement was quiet and thick with dust and history. "So what was suddenly so important down here?" Bev asked.

Lil pointed out a hump under the basement's concrete floor. "Look at that," she said.

"What you think it is, a body?" Bev asked jokingly.

"Actually, that would have been my thought, but it's growing."

Family Spirit

"Growing?"

"Yeah, it was closer to the wall a while ago, but now it's creeping more in here."

"It's the tree's roots," Bev said.

"I was hoping that's not what it is. That's major. The tree's gonna have to come down."

"Not on GG's watch it won't. You'd have a better chance taking down Luda's rainbow from the ceiling."

"Should we tell Dad?"

"No way. He'll try to uproot it and hurt himself in the process, or GG will hurt him for messing with her daddy's tree. So you really did need something," Bev said. "I thought you were trying to keep me from putting my foot up Carlotta's behind, since I rightly couldn't go after Aunt Helene."

"GG and Aunt Helene always settle their disputes," Lil said. "The fewer people all up in it to take sides and egg them on, the better."

"And that, my dear sister, like it or not, is why GG has you pegged to replace her. My mind just does not work like that."

The hostility had abated somewhat when they returned to the breakfast room. Flora was proposing an equitable rotation of the wearing of the Mother Ancestor's pearl. "Maybe Carlotta can wear it next time," she more pleaded than asked.

"That's not the point, the point is that GG doesn't get to call all the shots—" Helene said.

"Okay, so it's not about the pearl—" GG huffed.

"It is, but it's also about you and your ways—"

"Can you pick one, Helene? Though my preference is neither. We've just had an inspiring morning. Mrs. Baker has gotten uplifting news. The ancestors are smiling down on Carlotta for the way she yielded to the Knowing Spirit. Can we all just bask in that for a while longer?"

"Yes, please," Flora said, clapping her hands as murmurs of agreement rippled around the table, even from Helene's daughters and granddaughters. And Lil breathed a sigh of relief.

Lil managed to get out of the breakfast room, out of the house. But not before Helene commented on how tight Lil's jeans were. Bev rushed to point out that they were stretchy denim, they were supposed to be tight. Helene argued that there was no way Lil could get a panty girdle under those things, and the room erupted, especially from the younger girls.

Lil prepared to take flight, even as she had to listen to how Jesus was coming again because of tight dungarees. She taxied to the door. Once outside, she felt herself being lifted. Soaring with an open chest. She wondered if this was how Mr. Baker felt when he took that walk to nowhere. Her breaths were wide and deep, expansive. She had her grandfather's voice in her head, saying, "You can't do anything, Lillianna, if you don't first allow yourself to breathe."

8.

Are They Witches?

Lil didn't go to the library. Instead she went shopping for a peacoat to match the ones her two best friends, Lynn and Charise, had gotten. They were her only friends because she'd known them since they were all toddlers, so they were not put off by her family's strangeness. And even though Lynn's and Charise's parents would have preferred their children not love Lil so much, the girls did, and so they relented and allowed the friendships to blossom. Beyond them, Lil just had acquaintances. So many acquaintances, people liked being around her, tried to get close to her, but they could not get beyond the force field she'd constructed lest they get too close. Lest they hear it through the grapevine or see it for themselves that her family was cultish. Were they witches, devil worshippers, could they work roots and cause people to howl at the moon? She'd learned before she completed second grade that it was emotionally safer for her to hold even the sincerest-seeming people at a healthy distance—once they heard the blown-out-of-proportion stories about the Maces, they'd disengage from her. Except for her two friends who lived at either end of the block and called her house the center back, because it was in the center of the block and sat way back from the street.

Every year since they were old enough to shop for themselves, they'd made sure to buy one matching item of clothing emblematic of their bond. This year it was peacoats.

Lil acknowledged that her jeans were tight as she tried on a peacoat and stood in front of the mirror slanted against the wall at I Goldberg. She had slight shoulders and wide hips, and the cut of the jacket balanced her proportions. It felt right. Like it felt right to ditch the library today, and it felt right to switch her hips from side to side, giving the man who'd been eyeing her as he pretended to look at sweatshirts as good a view as she had of him through the slanted mirror.

He was wearing an aviator jacket with a gold chain peeking along the side of his crewneck sweater. He was cute in a boyish way, with his round face and big droopy eyes. He was clean-shaven, his hair cropped close, his mild brown complexion free of blemishes or razor bumps or worries.

He looked at her face and picked up her eyes through the mirror and smiled a closed-mouth smile. "Jacket fits you well," he said.

"You think?" she asked as she turned around to face him. "I like yours. And the reflection through the mirror doesn't do it justice."

"I would say the same about you, and not just the jacket," he added seamlessly. "I'm Kevin, by the way," he said, reaching into his breast pocket and pulling out a business card. "Just so that when I ask if I can have your number, you'll know I'm legit."

She glanced at the card. At the KYW logo embossed in the center. "Okay, you're a forward thinker, I see," she said, extending her hand. "I'm Lil. And I've got no business card to offer, so you're just gonna have to take my word for it."

"I'm willing to take the risk," he said, his eyes shining as he held her gaze.

He was bold, she thought, and smooth. She liked that. She didn't know if he was so appealing to her because he was cute, or because he worked at KYW and might be useful to her. "And what do you do at KYW? Surely not on-air talent, 'cause who wouldn't know that."

He blew a low-toned whistle. "On-air, me? You're right about that. I'm a behind-the-scenes brother. Production staff, Mike Douglas's show."

"Well, you could be in front of the camera if you wanted. You've got the look, as they say."

"No, Lil, you've got the look." He paused.

"Yeah? So put me on TV, then," she said as she shook her arms from the jacket. She had her grandmother's voice in her ear, saying, "Be direct about your wants. Life is too short for scheming." Lil knew she was doing both in this instance. "I'm a communications major. It would look good on my résumé."

"Let me buy you a cup of coffee and we can talk about it," he said. He helped her out of the peacoat and folded it over his arm.

"When you said, 'Let me buy,' I thought you talking about that." She motioned toward the jacket.

"I didn't think you'd accept such an offer."

"Pleeeze," she said, "you don't know me a little bit."

"Let's fix that, then," he said, smiling with an open mouth this time as she watched his eyes crinkle, joining in with the smile. She relieved him of the jacket and paid for it.

On her suggestion, they headed to the counter in Wanamaker's bargain basement, where he ordered a foot-long hot dog and chocolate milkshake, and she a grilled-cheese-and-tomato sandwich and coffee.

She chattered away as they ate, telling him about her dream of being a foreign correspondent so she could see the world on somebody else's dime.

"What's stopping you from going for it?" he asked, swiveling his stool in her direction so their knees touched.

"Stuff," she said. "Family stuff."

"Like husband-and-kids stuff?" he asked.

"Oh, hell no," she said, laughing, and she watched everything about him relax. "There's a lot going on with my family that I'm not gonna get into." She pulled at the tomato with her fork, freeing it from the confines of the bread and cheese. "But let's just say I'm kinda needed, and it sometimes interferes with the life I dream about."

"Well, you know, I don't think our dreams are supposed to come true, exactly; I think our dreams merely point us in a direction. So maybe you won't be a foreign correspondent, that doesn't mean you can't have work that might take you to Europe, Africa, Asia." He sipped his milkshake. He smiled and nodded. He was looking at her the way men often did, sizing her up, wondering about their chances, would she be easy or would they have to work for it. And if so, would she be worth the effort. Or was she too substantive for that to be even a consideration this soon. The answer also answered would she be worth it. She thought as she looked at his eyes, shining for her, that he could check all those boxes as a yes.

"To that end of baby steps," she continued, "I have an idea for a new segment of *The Mike Douglas Show*. Can I pitch it to you?"

"Ah, please do."

She sat up taller, allowing her knees to press further into his legs. "So it's called 'What Is Hip.'"

"Okay," he replied, amused.

"Yeah, so there would be a local correspondent, an unknown"—she cleared her throat in an exaggerated way—"such as myself. And so that correspondent would go around the city stopping people on the street, asking what is hip for them today and then encouraging them to tell a little story."

"Okay," he said, "got potential, elaborate, please."

"Well, the responses could be hilarious. An example: Today, if someone stopped me on the street and asked me, I would say my stretchy jeans are very hip."

"Oh, yes, they are," he said, said it emphatically.

She blushed; it was a feigned blush. "And if pressed to talk more, I would describe how my great-aunt told me my dungarees"—Lil air-quoted "dungarees"—"were too tight, and could I even get a panty girdle on under them."

His eyes turned to saucers, and then he laughed with an

open mouth. "Now, that is hilarious," he said, hitting his chest to recover himself.

"Right?" Lil continued. "And then my sister, a.k.a. my savior, rushed to say that they're supposed to be tight. Causing my older aunts to remark about how Jesus is coming again for sure."

"Wow, that's good stuff, Lil, it really is. Funny, original. But from my experience, most people won't be as quick and animated, and—might I add and hope I don't get myself into trouble here—as easy to look at as you are."

"Oh, please, everybody's easy to look at, especially if they're saying something that holds you. And the cutting room floor will make sure that happens."

"You've given this thought," he said.

She nodded. Actually, it was all from the top of her head. Though once he mentioned the thought she'd put into the pitch, she realized that she'd been thinking about this for some time, not this project, exactly, but a way out. This could be her way out. She could demonstrate to her grandmother that her time in school was not the ancillary busywork that GG regarded it as, just something to fill her time as she prepared to fulfill her purpose, according to her grandmother, of leading the family as they continued the bidding of the ancestors. Already she was seeing herself sitting down with GG, explaining there was not just one way to honor the ancestors, that she believed her talent and her purpose were in communicating, that she could use her talents to open hearts and bridge divides. She conceded she'd have to work on the clichés, give GG real-world evidence to make her points convincing. But if she could pull it off, surely GG would have to alter her succession plan. Carlotta was better suited for training to replace GG anyhow. She had a mean streak like GG. And if not Carlotta, surely Bev. Poor Bev. If only their mother weren't so damned fatigued all the time. Lil stopped herself. She felt guilty when she criticized her mother's condition, even if it was only to herself.

"Yeah," Kevin continued, "I respect the thought you've put into this. And I'm going to give it some thought, too. Of course, I don't have the standing that even approaches green-light powers—"

"Yet."

"Yet," he said, and, in acknowledgment, raised the tall, ribbed glass containing his chocolate milkshake. He took a sip, then tilted it in her direction, offering it to her.

"Whoa, hold on there, buddy, we just met," she joked. "Sipping from the same straw is moving pretty fast, that's at least third- or fourth-date stuff, don't you think?" They laughed then. It was an easy laugh, freeing.

She insisted on splitting the check, telling him that she didn't like to owe people. He insisted on walking her to the bus stop. "So now I've got to get your number so I can take you out on a proper date, and then a couple more after that so we can move toward sipping from the same straw," he said as they reached Walnut Street, and he pointed up the block to where he lived on Juniper near Spruce. He patted his pocket for a pen, then asked if she had one.

"No," she said, though she knew she had at least half a dozen pens in her oversize book bag.

"Well, can you wait here for like two minutes, and I'll jog up the street and grab one and be right back."

"Sure," she said.

"You promise you not gonna hop on the bus?" There was an unexpected pleading to his tone.

"How 'bout this," she offered. "How 'bout you walk instead of jog to where you live, and I'll walk with you."

"Let's do it," he said. "And this is gonna sound so old school in the corniest way, but since you got the bag with your new peacoat, can I carry your book bag for you?"

"Only if you promise not to judge me if one of my thousand pens comes falling."

✦ ✦ ✦

He walked her back to the bus stop after. She chattered away about the papers she was working on. She was cheery, as if what she'd just done—gone to an essentially strange man's apartment, watched his face fall in on itself as she undressed for him, then made his double-spring mattress sing to their beat—were an ordinary thing. When they reached Walnut Street, she asked when she could see him again, even though she knew her girlfriends would insist he should be the one doing the asking. But she could see that he was incapable right now, his brain still struggling to climb from where it had fallen when he'd seen her unclothed.

"Uh, when are you free?" he managed to reply finally. "You

just let me know. I mean, no, how about I call you. I'll call you to make sure you got home okay. Is that good? Can I, I mean, may I call you, Lil?"

"I'd love it if you did," she said as she watched her bus angle toward the curb. She tilted her chin so that he could brush his lips against hers. She settled into a window seat at the back of the bus and waved to him.

She looked out the window at the air growing fuchsia and gold as the sun prepared to set. She was seeing his naked walls that were absent artwork or framed family photos or even posters signed by guests whose appearances he'd helped arrange. His bed was similarly unclothed, no spread, or comforter, or quilt, or color beyond the beige sheets. His face had lost its color, too, caught up in the smoke from his bong. His complexion had veered from robustly oak-toned to a mild tan. When he cupped her face to kiss her, she tasted remnants of the milkshake he'd had, thick with chocolate syrup. After he pulled his sweater over his head, she lifted his undershirt to kiss his chest. There it was, the ID badge covered in plastic laminate. It was clipped to the bottom of his gold neck chain, so she hadn't seen it beneath his crewneck sweater. The plastic stuck to the perspiration dotting his skin as he pressed himself against her. Everything she'd seen during the ritual this morning was all there. The room with no color was there, the smoke from his bong, the taste of chocolate syrup when they kissed, the ID badge, both sticky and slick, was there, too.

The vision she'd had this morning was adding to itself as the bus jerked away from the curb. She felt as if she was floating, as if she was about to access that ephemeral space of timelessness, that airy and boundless place that she only went to under Luda's rainbow cocooned by her family's women as they danced and sang and helped her bring the foretelling to life. But here she was on a bus, a bus!

She closed her eyes as the vision took shape. "No." She said it emphatically, then repeated it, shaking her head. No. No. No. She could sense the people on the bus turning around to look at her. She didn't care. She was a Mace woman. Everyone thought them weird anyhow, family of crazies apt to zone out or start chanting in the middle of a conversation. Wore black velvet in the summer, white lace after Labor Day. Owned a pig, a pig! Refused to take their husband's last name when they gave their hand in marriage. And if you walked near their house around dawn and saw birds flying backward, you'd better cross the street before passing their front door or lightning would fall from the sky and strike you down dead.

She said no to the unfolding premonition the entire bus ride. Said no as she walked through the streets of her neighborhood filled with overgrown trees that were pulling up the pavement below them, and her thought was that the roots must be mammoth, the roots had the power to hit a gas line or otherwise disrupt foundational matter below the ground. The air was heavy as she walked, windless, exhausting. When she reached her house, depleted, she sat on the bottom step. She thought that she could feel the house pulsing beneath her feet as if it had a heartbeat, a soul. She put her head in her hands, still saying no, no, no.

Nona's Reading

October 2019, Nona's Writing Room, Philadelphia Exurbs

Nona wondered what Lil had just seen on that bus ride home as she slid her husband's cuff links into the slits of his bright white, severely starched sleeves. He was preparing for another extended rotation, twelve days, Europe. She thought he was traveling as much these days as Lil's father. Though Nona's husband, Bob, unlike Lil's dad, didn't have weird-ass in-laws he was trying to escape.

Maybe Lil's premonition had something to do with her dad, Nona thought, realizing that she needed to see Lil's father better. She figured he was fine like her husband was fine, with a facial structure that was both strong and soft, especially when he smiled and the drama of his cheekbones softened, enticing her to press her face against his.

She wondered if Lil's mother worried about her husband when he was on his too-frequent lengthy details. Did she imagine him flashing that smile for all the thirsty women he traveled with, women who shed their pulled-together workday attire and loosened up their attitudes for the scheduled evening events? She realized now that was why Hortense was always so tired, why she'd never become the family force she should have been given that she was GG's only daughter, why GG had reached beyond Hortense and scooped up Lil to train to manage the family when GG no longer could. She realized, too, that Hortense and Lil had the same desire: to run away. Hortense did manage to leave by staying, watching her husband do the same over and over and over again, breaking her heart.

When Nona finished with the cuff links, she pulled Bob's hand to her mouth and kissed it, letting her tongue swipe the skin.

"Don't be trying to start anything, lady," he joked as he nestled her into a hug. "I've got a plane to pilot."

"I know, I know," she said, pouting. Then reached up to straighten the golden wings she'd attached to his deep blue jacket.

The night before, she'd wrapped the wings and also the cuff links in fresh nettle leaves the way the fortune teller on South Street had directed. Nona didn't necessarily believe the nettle had any power, but the self-proclaimed soothsayer, Marlene, had charged Nona $29.99 for the leaves in addition to the cost of the reading; she said she had chanted over the leaves to heighten their power. "The nettle will repel no-good-doers," she'd said as she folded the leaves in black tissue paper and gently placed them in a bright yellow bag.

Everything in the small space of the shop was either yellow or black: the curtains, the scarves covering the rounded particleboard tables, the wall hangings that looked to be little more than construction paper scribbled on by preschoolers. Even Marlene's too-short caftan that exposed her knobby knees, and the bright rings on each of her index fingers, one ring shaped like a butterfly and the other a serpent, were yellow and black.

Nona asked Marlene about the colors as she looked at her, blond hair with screaming black roots. The skin on her face was remarkably smooth, tight; Nona wondered if she had a potion for that. Marlene responded with a laugh and said, "The yellow and black are for night and day."

"Night and day?"

Marlene just laughed again. Nona didn't like her laugh, the scratchy sound of it or the weight behind it, as if she held the answers to all the universe. The laugh said, *You crazy if you think I'm sharing my shit with you.*

Marlene had laughed when Nona first sat down and explained that she was there to discover if her husband was cheating on her because he traveled a lot for his job and had every opportunity. That wasn't why Nona was there. She was conducting research to determine how her depiction of the Maces lined up with someone purporting to predict the future in the real world.

Nona asked her what was funny, and Marlene straightened her back, cut the laugh off abruptly, and said, "I'm sorry, that's unprofessional of me, but I think you should be more concerned about your own fidelity, not his."

"I'm very faithful, I'll have you know," Nona said, insulted.

"Of course you are, dear, of course."

Nona hated to be called "dear," felt the person saying it was attempting to diminish her. She was about to say that she preferred to be called Nona, but before she could, Marlene held up her serpent index finger as if she were on a television set and had a producer in her ear telling her they were going live. Nona watched her close her eyes and inhale audibly. Nona breathed in deeply, too. The air in there smelled of a mix of lemon and pepper. She wondered if the manufactured aromas were meant to mimic and heighten the yellow and black color scheme.

She looked around the shop while Marlene sat as still as a bronzed statue of herself. The yellow paint was peeling at the seams where the walls met the ceiling. The painted floors were scuffed and showed hints of the pine beneath the black. The windows were coated in a fine layer of dust. Black and yellow balloons bounced happily against the dirty windows. She thought about the Mace home, its cared-for, respectful condition.

When Marlene opened her eyes, she leaned forward across the table and squinted at Nona's face as if she were a dermatologist looking for cancerous moles. "Yep, yep, yep," she said. "He's marked you."

"What are you talking about? Who?" Nona asked.

"Your husband. He's put your name on the altar. No matter what he does, you ain't going nowhere."

"He put my name on the altar? That makes no sense. I didn't ask about whether I would leave, anyhow; I asked about his fidelity."

"Look, sweetheart, and forgive me if me calling you 'sweetheart' heckles you as much as me calling you 'dear' got under your skin, because nomenclatures aren't important to me; it's the substance behind whatever we call a thing that matters. Similarly, the universe doesn't send me the answers to the questions you come in here asking; it sends me what you need to know, whether you're aware of the need or not. I don't have to continue, if that's your pleasure. The price is the same regardless, and I don't give refunds just because you don't want to hear your truth."

Nona watched Marlene take off her yellow and black snake ring and put it back on so that the snake's yellow eyes and its black tongue were pointed at Nona, seeming to move toward her as Marlene tapped her finger impatiently on the table. Nona backed off then. She didn't believe in spells per se, but she was petrified of snakes.

"Okay, so I'm listening to—to you, uh—to the universe."

Marlene told her then about the nettle, how to wrap something small that he'd wear during his travels in the nettle leaves the night before he was to put it on. And just as an aside, to keep his shoes pointed toward the bed, never toward the front door. She switched her ring back as she talked, so that Nona could see only the curve of the snake's tail.

"Okay, so, but you said there were things I didn't want to hear—"

Marlene replied with that laugh again. "Most people fear snakes," she said, and Nona held her face from showing her shock that this woman seemed to be reading her mind. "Yeah, I see you," she said, looking at Nona as if amused by her. "Everybody's got a snake inside them. Kind of slithering around unnoticed. That's a snake's power, you know, not its venom or its ability to squeeze the breath out of you or swallow a mammal many times wider than its girth. It's that it can be right there all the time, you know, and you going about your business, and then it goes hiss." She bared her teeth and moved her face closer to Nona's when she made the hissing sound, causing Nona to jump and release a yelp.

Marlene laughed again as she got up and went to the register. "You can pay now. And you shouldn't concern yourself so much with your husband's fidelity. A man's gonna man. The signals I'm getting say that you need to get yourself a flute and charm the snake that's waking up inside of you."

Nona left the worn-down shop with a heightened appreciation for the Maces and the way they conducted themselves. They were so earnest as they worked to understand whatever it was their seekers needed to know. They even put their bodies into it, causing themselves physical distress, as evidenced by what they went through after experiencing a Knowing. They'd so endeared themselves to Nona that she felt compassion even for the sniping Helene. She wanted to protect them. But the snake analogy from the mercenary Marlene did hold true. And she knew she had to allow the Maces to free themselves of their own serpents, reminding herself that they'd anchored themselves in God and the ancestors. She so envied their ability to do that.

9.
Private Dance

It had been two months since Lil had seen herself with the man in the colorless room. She'd vacillated between accepting it as a Knowing, that the man was in fact Kevin, or writing it off as pure coincidence. The accreted vision she'd had on the bus later that had spurred her incantations of "no, no, no" thankfully had not returned, and she'd consoled herself that it had been formed by meaningless fragments of her imagination because it happened outside the established ritual time, outside the power of Luda's rainbow centered above her, outside the reach of GG's calming arms, Bev's whispers of "You're okay, girl, let it out, let it go," even Carlotta holding her trembling hands to help her sip her tea.

She comforted herself now as she looked around Kevin's efficiency and noticed the hefty macramé floor pillow swirled in oranges and yellows and greens, the royal-blue ribbed bedspread, the bright red teakettle. Never mind that the items had been gifts from her, some splurges, some fantastic finds at Goodwill—the array of colors was a stunning visual departure from the room she'd seen during the ritual that morning. She looked at the pillow as she and Kevin sat together on the side of his bed, eating Chinese takeout on TV trays while watching *Saturday Night Live*. Kevin was laughing at "Weekend Update."

"That's some funny shit," he said when the commercial came on.

"It is, and you need to paint these walls."

"What's wrong with my walls?" he asked as he took her fork from between her fingers and put it on her plate and kissed her deeply, then laughed and said, "That was just my way of tasting that cashew chicken you're eating, since you're not sharing."

"Your walls are so bland. I'll help you paint," she said, picking up her fork in his plate to retrieve a piece of fried dumpling. "And just so you know, the kiss was nice, but you get more this way."

"But you get the sweetness from those pretty lips mixed in my way." His face went serious as he kissed her again.

She liked that, over two months in, he was still in the pinch-me-'cause-I-can't-believe-this-is-real phase: He'd still go dreamy-eyed at the first sight of her and stammer around as if he had to search for the word "hello." She'd been here before with men. Though generally, the more captivated they were by her, the more she felt the thrill ebbing, pulling her away. Not with Kevin. For the first time, she was returning a man's enthrallment with her in equal measure. Charise and Lynn joked with her that they had bets on how long this would last because she was going for some kind of record. They both gave him a thumbs-up, though, having met him when Lil brought him to a Black Student Union party at Drexel, where Lynn was a senior.

Lil thought she was going for a record as she kissed him back. They abandoned the cashew chicken and fried dumplings and *Saturday Night Live* and managed not to topple the TV trays as they pushed back on the bed and into each other.

They lingered. He traced her eyebrows with his fingers and kissed her nose, and she giggled. His new satiny sheets that she'd encouraged him to buy when they were last in Wanamaker's basement—their frequent special place because that was where they'd first broken bread together—were soft against her back, and she nestled into them and watched him looking at her as if he knew that her essential self was hidden under layers.

His voice was throaty as he started to speak. He managed to say only "So?" before he had to clear his throat and then cough away the phlegm. She felt bad for him that he was nervous, so she kissed him to try and arouse him again, to make him forget about what he was trying to say. Whatever he had to say that was stuck in his throat must be serious. She didn't want serious. She wanted to tickle him to make him laugh. Wanted to dance around his room and watch him watching her as she dipped and twirled and shook her butt. Wanted them to howl to stand-up comedy on HBO, or reruns of *The Beverly Hillbillies.*

She wanted to hear about his work, the stars he met at *The Mike Douglas Show*, wanted to hear about Michael Douglas himself, wanted to know if Kevin had mentioned her pitch for the "What Is Hip" segment to any of the higher-ups. She wanted to stay where they were in their relationship, on the shoreline, where the sand was warm under their feet. She didn't want to surf ocean waters that would pull her in deeper and deeper, didn't want to get all caught up in a riptide. She could go home if she wanted to feel like she had to struggle against monster waves that might take her down.

He pulled back from her overtures, sat all the way up. Rushed his words then. "I'm going home over break to Ohio to see my mom. I'd like for you to come. I told her about you, and she wants to meet you. And I want you to meet her."

He was shirtless, and she thought she could see his heart thumping hard under his breastbone, as if he'd just completed laps around Franklin Field. He looked at her, waiting, wanting.

"Aww," she said, dragging the word out as she laid her head against his chest. "That's so sweet, and I would love to meet your mom, but as I told you, I've got heavy-duty family stuff that keeps me lassoed to home."

"Actually, you haven't told me," he said as he sat up higher so that she had to sit up, too. "You say things like 'heavy-duty shit going on at home,' but what does that even mean?"

"It means what it sounds like," she said, not trying to hide the irritation creeping into her tone as she braced herself for the "When you gonna invite me to your house to meet the folks?" question that her previous boyfriends had asked, at

Family Spirit

which point she'd always found a way to break it off. So far Kevin hadn't asked. Just said that he felt like she was always hiding behind her family's issues.

"Every family's got issues," he said as he got up. "I'mma take a shower." And just like that, he was on the other side of the bathroom door. He always asked her to join him in the shower. He didn't tonight.

She swallowed the lump in her throat, insisting to herself that she was not going to cry; he didn't mean that much to her for her to be crying over him. Even though she really did want to cry. He did mean that much to her.

She punched her books and clothes into her overnight bag and slipped out while he was in the shower. She'd driven here in the family's station wagon. The gas tank was on E, though; Kevin had planned to fill it for her in the morning and also change the oil.

A mile from home and she felt the wagon sputtering. She coasted to the curb and the car stopped. She hit the steering wheel; she shouted fuck; she fished through her bag for a token for the trolley. It was after midnight; the trolley ran irregularly after midnight. She leaned back against the headrest and took in deep breaths to calm herself. She couldn't do anything if she couldn't breathe. Had her grandfather's voice in her head saying as much.

There was a church on one corner, a bar on the other. Both were aglow with activity, music and foot stomping informed by spirits flowing in the one, the Spirit moving in the other. Both would likely have a pay phone. Whom would she even call.

She knew Lynn and Charise were unavailable. They'd gone to Florida for Florida A&M University's homecoming.

If her father were home, he'd come get her, no questions asked except "You okay?" Those were always his first words to her. Not hello, not how've you been, what's been going on. It didn't matter if he'd been away for weeks. "You okay?" He'd wait for her reply, taking in her presence as if looking for clues on how she would respond, as if preparing himself for her not being okay. She'd always respond, "Yes, Daddy, I'm okay," because upon seeing him, finally, she always was, even if she had not been just a moment ago. Then a palpable relief would overtake him. She'd realize how much he likely worried about them all when he was away—her mother, Bev, Miles, likely GG, too—as he'd spread his arms for Lil to fall into.

But he wasn't home.

She'd have to settle for Bev and the schooling she'd likely get about how important it was to have a plan B when you were out with a man. *Parking your car at his house on empty is not even a plan Z, not even the alphabet,* she'd say. As irritating as Bev could be when she got preachy, Lil still knew that Bev was her ace. They trusted each other fiercely. Bev covered for Lil without hesitation on nights like this. "Lil was on campus late, so she slept over at her classmates'," she'd tell GG if GG came looking for Lil.

Lil was deciding between the church and the bar for a pay phone. Both had their perils. The hooting men in the bar would try to buy her drinks, try to talk her into going home with them; the people in the church would encourage her to praise God the way they did, with shouts and frenzy, hoarse and exhausted until past midnight.

She decided on the church. She exchanged her token for a quarter and prepared herself to face the music with Bev, who she knew would come right away for her in their father's like-new five-year-old red-inside-and-out Monte Carlo, the car his alter ego because he was otherwise low-key.

Lil put her overnight bag down on the floor, out of view. When she looked up, she saw a woman leaving the church. She was dressed like a go-go girl from the 1960s, with her red-flowered miniskirt and copper-toned patent-leather boots and waist-length denim jacket. She was so thin that Lil thought even a light gust of air would carry her away, helped along by her massive hair, which had already taken flight, going in every direction as if it had been randomly raked through and then let be. Lil watched her cross the street. A fine mist hung in the air like stardust and bounced with the woman as she moved, as if her copper-colored boots walked on clouds instead of concrete, floating her toward the bar. When she opened the door, red and blue lights and laughter and loud talk gushed out and then, as if realizing they had no purpose out here, reversed course and pulled the woman and her sheen inside.

Lil reversed course, too, and rode the gushing red and blue into the bar. The air dripped with sweat and whiskey and desire. Already the woman was on the small square of dance floor, moving her thinness to the beat of James Brown hollering "I Feel Good." Her head was thrown back, her mouth open. She was a natural dancer, like Michael Jackson. All her inflections from her foot moves in her copper go-go boots to her finger curls to what she did with her eyebrows were in sync, to the beat, with feeling, with meaning, like good poetry. Lil had never seen anyone dance like this, and she stood there, gawking. Everyone else in here—crowded at the bar, crammed in at the tables meant for four people where there were at least six—was oblivious to her talent.

But Lil was so mesmerized by her, she didn't even resist when the woman reached her arm through the red and blue lights and the sweaty air and loud talk and good times and snatched Lil onto the dance floor. She pulled Lil to her, put her arms around her neck, and Lil touched either side of her waist gingerly, afraid that the woman might break if held too tightly. She smelled sweet, like talcum powder, and they commenced to slow-drag to James Brown's fast song. She pulled her head back and looked at Lil and smiled. It was a soft, sweet smile, the way someone would smile at a newborn. "You cute," she said to Lil. "How old are you?"

"Twenty-one," Lil said.

"My daughter's a little younger than you, but she cute like you."

Lil nodded. "You're cute, too," she said. "And you can really dance. And did I see you leaving the church across the street?"

"Yeah, chile. I dance over there, too. They got some smooth foot workers over there. They got a holy dance that gives me a run for my money. I can't even keep up with them in my go-go boots. Aren't my boots sharp? I want to be buried in them. You got a good mother?"

"Uh," Lil said, then hesitated. She didn't know why she hesitated; of course Hortense was good. She was just always so exhausted. "She's a real good mother," she said, "just tires easily."

"I hope she's not sick. Hard being sick when you got kids." She looked beyond Lil and waved. "That's my man, coming to take me home. He's a deacon 'cross the street. He can cut a rug, too, both in here and over there." She pulled Lil all the way to her and hugged her tightly. Lil thought she could feel her bones through her denim jacket, as if nothing covered them save the jacket. She kissed Lil hard on the cheek. "Love you, doll," she said.

"Love you, too," Lil said as the woman switched her smallness toward the man waiting for her in a plaid-on-plaid suit and red fedora, head tilted, a misty expression on his face. The man took her hand and led her out. Already Lil missed her.

Nona Breaks It Down

December 2019, Nona's Writing Room, Philadelphia Exurbs

After Nona watched Lil walk into the bar and dance with the woman who was too thin, she took a writing break. She didn't know where the woman came from, and she didn't have time for unrelated objects disguised as nuggets falling from the sky. This was no nugget falling from the sky. This was a distraction that presented itself as snow and engaged her imagination, spurring her on to depict the softness of snow, the astounding silence of its magical twirls like poetry falling. But this was not snow. This was hail. An anomaly of hard white balls that meant nothing and did nothing, added nothing.

The scene would have made sense if Lil had no mother. But Lil had Hortense. Admittedly, Hortense wasn't the most emotionally available mother; she was always tired, likely depressed. Probably experiencing perimenopause. But Hortense's pathology, such as it was, did not warrant Lil's hunger for the connection that she seemed to have with the woman in the bar. Plus, Lil had better than a mother in GG; and she had her older sister, Bev. She'd always been attached to substantive, endearing women.

Nona knew that once she started analyzing the whys and wherefores of that scene, she'd become a small sparrow in a large cage, with enough room to spread its wings and take short low-lying flights but then coming to the heartbreaking realization that it could never be free to soar.

So Nona would take a break to reclaim her focus. Bob would be home tomorrow, and her cousin and her cousin's grandchildren were coming over to go to a nursery where they'd ride a sleigh through the woods to find their perfect Christmas tree and cut it down and bring it home to decorate. Bob would build a fire and roast marshmallows with the kids. She and her cousin would prepare pans of yeast rolls and jars of applesauce using the recipes passed down from their grandmother, spoken-word recipes that they'd repeat step by step as they formed the dough and boiled the apples, laughing and swiping at tears soaked with memories.

Nona was looking forward to tomorrow. A good day to turn away from the page, a good distraction. Not like the distraction of a random woman showing up in a bar to dance with Lil.

Her phone buzzed and a text message glowed from Bob.

Snowed in. Horrific backup. Lucky if I can make it out of here by tomorrow night.

She hit the phone icon to call him. Voicemail. "Dammit," she said so loudly she startled even herself. She banged her fist on the desk and felt the pain ratchet up her arm. She massaged her hand, then went to the freezer for an ice pack. She thought she could still have the date with her cousin and the kids. Though she surely wasn't about to chop down a tree, and even if the nursery people took it down for her, she wasn't trying to lug a big-ass tree into the house. And Bob was so good with the kids.

She pressed the ice pack around her hand. The jolts of pain in her hand and her arm began to subside. Not the disappointment, though. She felt the disappointment in her stomach as cramps moved from her back to her abdomen. She felt anger mixing in: at Bob for talking her into moving all the way out here to these hinterlands filled with people stockpiling survival kits for the revolution; at herself for agreeing, even though she'd known he'd have an erratic schedule and would often be gone at night and over weekends; and at herself for neglecting to get more nettle to wrap Bob's cuff links in, and his shiny gold wings, as the snake-ring-wearing fortune teller with the hideous laugh suggested that she do.

10.

The Pickup After the Private Dance

Lil wiped away tears as she watched the too-thin woman in the go-go boots leave the bar. She didn't know what about her caused the tears. Insisted to herself that it had nothing to do with Kevin. She steadied her voice as she used the bar's pay phone to call Bev, to explain that the wagon had run out of gas, could she please come pick her up.

Bev arrived quickly. She had Miles with her; he was sound asleep in the back in his car seat. "I tried to wake Mama to tell her to keep an ear out for Miles," Bev whispered so as not to wake Miles, "but you know she's dead to the world once she closes her eyes. I didn't want him to wake up and start howling with no one to answer his cries save GG, which would cause a whole 'nother set of problems 'cause she'd want to know where the hell we were."

"I appreciate it," Lil said, adding that she also appreciated Bev for not giving her shit for riding around with an empty gas tank.

Once they were all in the house and Miles was resnuggled in his bed, Bev told Lil that her guy had called three times already. "Lovers' spat and you left while he was in the shower?" Bev asked.

"He told you that?" Lil said, aghast.

"No, he didn't told me that," Bev imitated Lil. "I just know you. And I'm guessing he's the latest in your string of good brothers who want to meet the fam but you not ready to get that serious?"

"So what if that's the case, what's wrong with it?" Lil said. "I don't see you rushing to bring anybody to meet the fam." Now she imitated Bev.

"I don't have to," Bev said. "My guys are here regularly. The mailman, the milkman, the bread man."

"Shut the hell up," Lil said. "We don't even have a bread man or a milkman."

"Ah, true, little sis, but we do have a mailman, and let me tell you, boyfriend delivers." Bev laughed as she fanned herself and followed Lil into her bedroom. Then she told Lil, "Call the boy, he sounded worried."

"I'm not calling him; I'm going to take a shower," Lil said as she stepped out of her shoes and pulled off her sweater.

"See, you could have taken one with him," Bev said, and Lil balled up her sweater and threw it at Bev. Bev ducked and laughed as she left Lil alone in her room.

Kevin called Lil repeatedly for the next week. She refused to take his calls. Convinced herself that she was too busy to be navigating a relationship with someone who wanted too much from her, wanted to mire her in the quicksand of family entanglements. She managed not to think about him, at least not much. She kept herself well occupied. Took Pig to his regular frolic at Ridley Creek State Park, served as notetaker for two separate families: one seeking the whereabouts of their Alzheimer's-suffering grandfather, the other seeking guidance on whether to pursue an appeal in a costly medical-malpractice lawsuit. Her father returned once again, and she and Bev joined him for a daddy-daughters night out complete with a Patti LaBelle concert followed by their favorite childhood treat, a juicy cheeseburger and a float with Coke. Twice she rode by the spot where the wagon had run out of gas. She parked at the corner and watched people come and go from the church and the bar. The air was never right. No mist that fell like stardust, no waves of red and blue gushing from the bar, no glowing yellow light escaping from the church. So of course she didn't see the woman who'd danced with her and kissed her cheek and called her doll. She hadn't expected to. She just wanted to be close to where she'd been so she could continue to absorb the idea of her.

✦ ✦ ✦

As much as Lil tried to tell herself that Kevin meant little to her, she had in fact been counting the days since the night she'd left his apartment. Sometimes she had to remind herself exactly what he'd done—could it have really been that horrible if she had to search around for the provocation? And then she'd remember. He wanted to take her home to meet his mother; he wanted an explanation for why she couldn't go. Oh right, she'd remind herself. Fuck you then, Kevin. She'd feel justified.

But on her way to class, she heard him call out to her. She had just exited the bus and was rushing up the stairs to the El platform to catch her train. The sound of her name with his voice attached to it flying through the unseasonably warm air, the pleading to the tone, stopped her, softened her. Now she remembered how much she'd missed hearing him call for her, and she turned around and slowly descended the few steps to be on level ground where he stood. She resisted the feel of the air wrapping itself around her, constricting her. She thought the air was trying to tell her something, and she didn't want to listen. Except it wasn't the air wrapping around her. It was his arms encased in his suede jacket, holding her close, and she yielded to this constriction because the suede was tender against her face as she pressed her head against his chest. She deferred her worry about what the tightness in the air meant for the next moment and the ones to follow. Right now she allowed her whole self to sigh into him, and after a moment, he took her hand and walked her to his car and opened the door for her to slide into the passenger seat. "Be right back," he said, "gotta hit the little boys' room."

His new Volvo was its usual immaculate self, save two empty coffee cups stacked, and she wondered how long he'd been waiting in his car for her to finally appear. Generally, she would have been here an hour and a half ago, but her first class had been canceled. He knew her schedule because they'd had a blowup about it—actually, she'd blown up—not long ago, when she'd complained how crazy she must have been to have registered for such an early class, and how she had to hustle to get to the El because the trolley was always late, but she had to take a bus to get to the El. He said that she should just drive to the El and park. She explained that she didn't want the hassle of looking for parking spaces on overcrowded Market Street. "Well, you should just get someone else in your house to drop you off," he'd said, as if that were the easiest thing in the world for her to do. Her mother didn't drive, Bev was already saddled with getting Miles to day care, and then, depending on her mother's energy level, Bev would have to pick up her mother's slack as well as work through whatever Bev-do list GG had constructed. Lil would not add an iota more to Bev's responsibilities unless it was an absolute emergency. She'd erupted at him then. Told him she wasn't looking for his what-she-should-do solutions. She was venting, that's all, about herself signing up for such an early class, about Philly's transit system, about her classes not being available at Temple's satellite campus in Center City. The only part of him that her whole rant involved was his ear, that's all. She'd just needed his ear, not his advice, not his commentary, not his questions about her household.

When he got back in the car, she asked if he'd been waiting there for a while, and she pointed to the empty coffee cups.

"You're a perceptive one, yes. And I promise one of those coffees was for you, but it was getting cold," he said.

"I'm sorry, my first class was canceled."

"I figured something like that happened. I was just hoping everything was okay or that you hadn't changed your route—"

"Nope, didn't change my route," she said.

"What have you changed?" he asked. Then he rushed to say please forget that he'd just asked that. His intent wasn't to pull her into a whole heavy conversation about the status of their relationship or lack of one.

"No, it's okay," she said as she nestled into the leather seat. "It's so good to see you, I'mma just let it go."

He looked away, looked at the hustle and bustle outside the window. "I can see why you're not trying to find parking near here. I'm so spoiled because I get to walk to work, you know."

"Oh yeah, I know, you got walking man's privilege." She laughed, he did, too. "So, you stalking me for a reason, or you just wanted to say hi? I mean, either is cool."

He sat up then as if he'd suddenly remembered why he was there. "Oh hell yeah, there's a reason, a very good reason, I'm out here stalking you when I should be at work. Beyond just wanting to see you, I have news, promising news. At least I think it's promising."

"I'm listening," she said as she angled toward him.

"Well, as it turns out, I took your 'What Is Hip' pitch to my boss—actually, it was a while ago, but I didn't want to tell you until I had something to tell other than, you know, I'd talked to my boss about it."

"Okay," she said calmly. Though she thought she'd actually stopped breathing, because the sound of her breath was getting in the way of her hearing.

"He said it's got potential."

"Potential, what's that mean? I mean not the word, of course, but in the context of him saying it."

"It means just that. It's a good-ass idea, and there are signs of life," he said.

"Wow, that's incredible. I mean, with me? You know, you pitched it with me as the one interviewing the people on the street?"

"Of course that's how I pitched it. I mean certainly there will be a few hoops for you to jump through, but who wouldn't love you? I mean, damn, you're such a natural." He looked at her, then looked away as if it hurt to look at her.

"Oh my God, this is huge."

"Trust me, it is," he said. "I mean that he even listened beyond the initial elevator pitch and asked me to do a whole proposal is, in and of itself, huge."

"So where is it, the proposal, is it still with him? Will Mike Douglas have the final say?"

"Mike Douglas will weigh in, but he generally thumbs-ups what his senior producers bring him. That's why it's such a big deal, my boss took it to the production meeting and got some positive signals."

"Wow, so who's the decider who takes it to Mike Douglas?"

"It sure as hell ain't me, or it would have been a done deal weeks ago." He laughed, and she did, too. Though she thought it a serious question.

"Well, it should be you," she said, stroking his ego; she also stroked his hand resting on top of the gearshift. "And in a fair world, it would be you. So what do I need to do? Who do I meet with there? Oh my God, there'll be contracts, I need representation, right?"

"Actually, no."

"No?"

"They want to of course meet you. And the plan is to bring you on as a student intern. That way they can put you on-air as part of the training program without all the rigmarole of contracts, agents, you know, the legal stuff will take forever, but you still get the benefit of the experience and, probably more important, the exposure. The intern program is legit," he said as he named the other schools they'd worked with, "Penn, Drexel, La Salle, Penn State, you know, you won't be exploited, I promise you. Plus, you get a nice stipend."

"Daaamn, this is a lot to process," she said.

"It is, I know. And I'm hearing they want to move quickly. It's so worth it, though; imagine how helpful the tapes will be for your job search." He paused and looked at her, then said, "I hope this works out." He brought her hand to his lips and kissed it.

"Me too," she said, even though she wasn't sure what he was hoping would work out, her "What Is Hip" idea or their relationship. Though she knew that the two were so intertwined, so symbiotic, one likely couldn't exist without the other.

She had her grandmother's voice in her head, saying it was dangerous to want something too much, that kind of wanting will disrupt your peace, take you over, pull you under, have you going left when you should go right, and in the end leave you looking and feeling like a fool. She knew this was something that she wanted so much, but not too much, she convinced herself as Kevin leaned in to rub his lips against hers. She parted her mouth and released a whisper of a moan and said she could take the day off from class, could he from work? Please, could he.

"God, yes indeed I can," he said as he kissed her harder, then put his car in drive and pulled away from the curb.

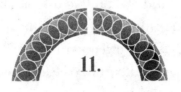

11.

Jealousy

She thought she was falling in love with Kevin after news of the proposal's potential. Even though she'd never considered herself the falling-in-love type, the type to become the personification of clichés, dreamy-eyed over a man, walking on clouds, acting like a brainless zombie. But here she was with him on her mind all the time, calling him at work just to say hello, skipping class to be with him, planning her outfits based on what she thought he'd like. Even her barely aware mother asked what the heck was going on with her when Lil pressed out her hair. And Lil always loved her hair in its natural state, its crinkled density, like Luda's. Bev shook her head when she saw Lil's hair long and limp, curls having been pressed into submission. "I guess this Kevin is the one, but if you go blond, I'mma have to step to him."

Lil was oblivious to other people's reactions. Only his reaction mattered. Pleasing him became so paramount that she agreed to go to Ohio with him to meet his mother. She'd told Lynn and Charise, and they asked her over and over, wasn't that why they'd broken up in the first place, because she didn't want to take that trip. "Traveling all that way to meet the mom sounds like a big step," Lynn insisted.

"Yeah, like a serious-commitment kind of a step," Charise added. "Trading your family for his, in a way."

Lil told them that she had drawn the line. That she wouldn't take the road trip with him both ways. She'd fly back solo so she could spend Christmas morning with her family, especially with Miles. It wouldn't be Christmas without Miles.

Over the next days, Lil held herself from asking about the "What Is Hip" project. She trusted Kevin. Realized that she'd never trusted a man she was seeing. She'd never let anyone in enough for trust to be a factor, to be necessary. But now it was necessary. It became necessary the night she went with him to a party around the corner from where he lived.

It was a hodgepodge gathering of people he knew loosely from his neighborhood, mostly white boys with a few Black people sprinkled in. Lil turned her attention to one woman with lips fuller than Lil's, bigger legs, smaller waist, shapelier behind, all on display in the stretchy pencil skirt and crop top she wore even though it was November outside and chilly in the expansive third-floor apartment, too. Lil thought the woman was overtly coming on to Kevin. She'd been here before, had been generally amused when women eyed the man she was with. Her attitude had always been *Go for it, sister.* It was too easy for Lil to say bye to men. No hurt feelings, no resentments: As her friend Lynn would joke, "Lil's real quick to end a relationship with 'It's been real and it's been fun, but I can't say it's been real fun.'" This time last month, Lil would have had the same reaction to this woman, with her mile-long fingernails on Kevin's arm, asking him didn't she see him all the time at H. A. Winston's. She was a server there, and if it hadn't been him, he must have a good-looking identical twin.

"I confess, it's me," Kevin said, "their chili is my go-to dinner."

"Their chili is incredible," Lil said, not looking at the woman because she was sure she wouldn't be able to contain the glare, and she didn't want to show herself as petty.

She was feeling something new, something she'd never understood when she'd heard the feeling described by Lynn or Charise or the women who came to see GG with questions about their marriage or relationships. A composite rage; a seething mix of fear and resentment, of haughty belligerence; an unchecked stew of want boiling over, warping surfaces unprepared for its onslaught. Where did this want for him come from so suddenly? What was it about him that had her unraveling like this because another woman was talking to him? Even as she asked herself this, another question was trying to elbow its way into her consciousness. A question that deleted Kevin from the equation, a question that ignored the fast-forward woman with her foot-long nails on his arm. GG always said, "It's hard to get the right answer when you're asking the wrong question."

Right now Lil shrugged all the questions away, right, wrong, or indifferent. Then she walked away. Switched her hips across the room, hoping they'd garner attention, hoping Kevin might feel an inkling of what she did in the moment. She heard him laughing at something the Winston waitress said. Had he even noticed she'd left his side?

She went into the bedroom, where the dresser was serving as a bar. A trio of men bent over the nightstand, doing lines of coke. She poured wine into a plastic cup and swallowed it all in just a few gulps. Then she did it again. She looked at herself in the mirror and wondered who she even was in this moment. She certainly wasn't a drinker, and she felt the wine climb immediately to her head.

Just as she looked around for someone to make small talk with, preferably a man she could dazzle for a few to distract herself from herself, a six-feet-tall woman with hoop earrings hanging from her nose, and gold and silver chains hanging around her neck, and shaved eyebrows, though otherwise model-stunning like Iman, handed her a joint. Lil smiled at the woman and accepted the joint and pulled on it and tried to hold the smoke. She started coughing as she handed the joint back to the woman. She didn't do much weed, either.

"What's your name, cutie?" the woman asked.

"Lil," she said, trying to hold the rest of the cough in.

"I'm Max, Lil. You with the dude the sister in the spandex is in there hitting on?"

Lil hunched her shoulders. "Define 'with,'" she said. "We're not married, not even engaged."

"Now, that's not what I'm asking you, sweet Lil. Did you come here with him?"

"I came here with him, yeah." She took the joint again and pulled on it, though not as hard this time.

"You've got some pretty lips, Lil."

"Thanks, so do you, Max. In fact, your whole face is, like, ravishing. But I know you hear that all the time. Do agents stop you on the street offering you modeling contracts?"

"Yeah, happens a lot," Max said nonchalantly. "But back to you, Lil. You are aware that just 'cause you came in here with him doesn't mean you have to leave with him. You could make a fabulously bold statement by blowing him a kiss and going back out that door with someone else." She raised her non-eyebrow suggestively.

"I'm good, Max, thanks for the offer, though," Lil said, then smiled a closed-mouth smile.

Max exaggerated a pout. "Boo-hoo, that makes me so sad," she said. "I could teach you some things. But at least let me give you a parting gift to help you deal with the asshole you might or might not be here with." She pulled on her thick neck chains: One had a spoon on the end; the other was a locket. She motioned Lil to the dresser. She dipped the spoon in the locket and spread two lines of coke on the dresser. She offered a metal straw to Lil. "Just breathe how you would breathe if your nose is stopped up and you're taking a nasal spray."

"Okay, Super Fly," Lil said as she listened to Max giggle.

Lil had never tried cocaine; she was never in the sets where it was even available, and if it was available, she was oblivious. She didn't especially want to do it now, but she wasn't averse to it, either. She thought maybe it was the wine she'd gulped, the tokes of weed she'd taken, her fury at Kevin, Max's engaging personality. She said what the hell and did as Max instructed and breathed the powder up her nose.

She didn't know what to feel, so she was surprised that she felt nothing. She watched Max inhale her portion. Watched her sniff hard, watched her face go intense as she sniffed, watched one side of her gorgeous face go incongruent with the other, making her face suddenly unbeautiful, and then watched her features go symmetrical again as everything about her perfect face fell back into place. Max's eyes were focusing again, and Lil saw a flash of disappointment darken her face as she looked beyond Lil, and Lil knew Kevin had entered the room.

"Oh, so you found the quiet room," Kevin said as he put his arm around Lil and kissed her cheek. Then he extended his hand as Lil introduced him to Max.

"Y'all have a good night," Max said, then pushed through the quiet jazz back into the loud music in the front.

12.

Yosemite Falls

As soon as Kevin closed the door and put all five locks on, Lil pulled her hair down from its upsweep and pulled out moves she didn't even know she had with such ferocity that she rendered him a helpless sycophant, following her every lead, trying to keep up as he gasped and held on.

"Damn, baby," he said after, still trying to catch his breath. "Damn."

She looked at his eyes, shining for her as if she were a marvel. Suddenly she wanted him to have all of her, to know all of her. She leaned in and kissed him, then said, "I've got something to tell you."

"What, that you are the best of the best? I mean, wow," he said.

She was on one elbow, looking down at him. "I've got powers," she said.

"Oh hell yeah, you do," he said as he reached up to stroke her lips.

Family Spirit

"I'm serious, I've got real powers."

She felt her heartbeat step up the way it had when she was all over him. Her words fell quickly to keep up with her heartbeat. She talked faster, trying to sync her words with her thoughts, which were forming in torrents, gushing now like a great waterfall, like Yosemite, where the indigenous dwellers said witches lived. She felt like a witch was inside her now, working a spell on her as words rushed down, bringing her secrets to gleam atop the dramatic plunge of water foaming, changing colors, green and purple and blue exploding in mists. What a display her words made. They were impossible to look away from, impossible not to hear.

"I can see things, many of the women in my family can, too. We're clairvoyant; it's an inherited thing. We call it Knowing. We have rituals to help each other experience Knowings. Very elaborate affairs, with amazing attire, handsewn, intricate, oh my God, so fucking beautiful. But it takes a lot, our practice, and we help people, you know, people pay, but we're ordained by God and our ancestors to give the seekers who come to us what it is they need to know.

"We're real specific with our practice. Which is why I don't bring people to my house, especially men, it's complicated with the men. They have their own ritual that I'm not privy to. I just know if I were to bring home a suitable prospect, the other men would take him wherever they take him, and school him, and initiate him. And no one would ever talk about it, they don't talk about it, but I think it's kind of brutal, because the men have to be the backbone, you know, the women are the heart, but the men got to bring their strength.

"And it's a lot of responsibility, you know, for everybody. And my sister and I, I mean we really feel the responsibility because we live with our grandmother and she's the center, she keeps things moving, she's incredible, as I talk, I'm realizing how fucking incredible she is. She holds the whole thing down."

Lil was crying as she gushed about GG, how much she loved her, how devoted she was to her. "My grandmom can sense who's going to be the one to break out and experience the Knowing. She just knows shit, about people, about things, about the fucking universe."

Lil was sobbing now.

"But it's a lot, which is why when it seems like I'm unavailable, I really am unavailable. But it's my life right now. I hate that it's my life, but I love it, too, you know, my family, my community, I love that part of it, but I fucking hate it, too. And my grandmother wants me to be her. But I can't be her, you know. She wants me to take over for her, and that's just too large of a thing to ask from me. But she's determined, and I can't find a way to tell her that I can't or, more truthfully, that I don't want to. I want to see the world, you know. I want to experience things that have nothing to do with seeing into another person's tomorrow so that I can honor Luda, our ancestor. Luda saw a rainbow fall from the sky and proclaimed a similar future for every girl child born to a Mace. Luda, it's all about honoring Luda. I want to, but I can't because I also don't want to."

She was crying, talking so fast she didn't even realize at first that she'd actually said Luda's name out loud, that cov-

Family Spirit

eted name they uttered only among themselves, the name that, as children, they never even heard the adults verbalize. This name was so sacred it was breathed only within their circle, in reverence, in prayer.

But she'd just said it as naturally as if she'd been saying her own name. And then she felt nothing. No remorse, no inclination to rush in and reverse what she'd just said. To stop. She couldn't stop. The rush of the waterfall was too heavy, she had to hang on to its outer edge, its foam, because the center would crush her. So she rode the water down, down, to the foot of the Yosemite, where they said the witches lived. She wished she could trade her power for theirs. Wished that she could use their power to make her power disappear.

Kevin inched up higher and higher in the bed as she talked. By the time she finished, he was sitting straight up, his mouth agape, a new intensity to his jawline. His eyes searched her face, as if he was trying to know for sure that she was telling the truth, that she wasn't just fucking with him and in a minute was gonna start laughing and yell *Sike!*

She'd never felt so vulnerable as she waited for him to say something. She realized in that moment what a protective life she'd had, cocooned from real danger by the very family she oftentimes resented because of the expectations they placed on her. God, her family, her remarkable family. What had she just done. She'd just breached the sacred trust they put in her, in each other. Now she wanted to recall what she'd said, wanted to reach into Kevin's mind and reclaim her words and erase them from his memory and run home to GG and snuggle in her bed the way she used to when she was young and had a bad dream. But he was already buzzing with questions, so many questions, as if he were a beat cop trying to work his way up to detective and overasking so he wouldn't leave anything out.

"I mean, could you predict my future?" he asked. "Could I come to witness a ritual? Am I gonna get a promotion? I mean, how do you know that it's a, I guess, a vision? Do you see like a whole scene, or is it more like symbolic?"

"I'm exhausted," she said as he ticked off an endless stream of questions. "We can talk about this in the morning."

She curled up on the bed. He folded himself around her and kissed her cheek and whispered, "Sleep tight, baby."

She could feel his heart pounding against her back. What did I just do? she asked herself. Sweet Jesus, what did I just do?

✦ ✦ ✦

The way it was supposed to work was that the Maces never discussed their clairvoyance outside the family; they never affirmed nor denied their gift. They accepted the whispers, the avoidance, the slights, sometimes even taunts, as standard territory. They considered themselves special, exalted, so that the swipes from people who didn't know enough to know were irritants, like gnats, that could be easily controlled with something sweet in an uncovered bowl that they'd dip into and get stuck and drown. The seekers who came to them were by referral from other people the Maces had helped.

"I know a woman," an empathetic listener might say to a

neighbor confiding that she was unsure about having a hysterectomy for fibroids; or the mother of a child's best friend confessing that her oldest son was on that stuff, should she let him back into the house; or a regular at the hair salon wondering if her husband had a whole 'nother family in Hackensack; or a coworker who had been offered a position that would mean relocating to Albuquerque, New Mexico; or a cousin who thought their white-bro boyfriend might be in the Russian mob; or a car mechanic who was considering a franchise opportunity with Pep Boys; or a receptionist at a dentist's office deciding about a lumpectomy or mastectomy for the just discovered mass. All needed the direction, insight, foresight, a vision, a gleam of the substance of what was to come, something to believe in. Because at some point, even the most agnostic needed something they could trust, and even the most devout lost faith in what had worked and needed a momentary new thing to cling to.

They'd show up on the porch of the house. And even at dawn, when the first light revealed core truths, a Mace woman would still neither affirm nor deny her gift to a person not part of their tribe. "We'll see" was GG's typical response when a seeker asked if she could help. "We'll see."

And never, ever would they invoke Luda's sacred name, as Lil had just done.

The next morning Kevin was uncharacteristically up before Lil. He'd already gone to the corner and picked up the Sunday paper and splurged on fresh-squeezed orange juice. Grits were bubbling in the pan, and he was cracking eggs when she got into the kitchen. He pulled her to him and pressed her close with a new intensity. "I'm making my beautiful baby some breakfast this beautiful morning," he said.

"That's sweet," she said. "Can I do anything?"

"Maybe throw some bread in the toaster oven. And then get comfortable, 'cause I'm serving you today. Plus, I want to hear more about what you were telling me last night."

"About that," she said, "I had too much to drink at the party, and I had a hit of cocaine from that Max person, so I was basically talking shit."

"Really?" He put down the egg he was about to crack and looked at her.

"What are you asking about, me talking shit or the cocaine?"

"I didn't know you were into blow, but I mean it's cool, I've dabbled now and then, no biggie. But I was saying really about you saying you were just talking stuff about the whole clairvoyance. And your family and everything. I mean, wow."

"Well, really," she said emphatically.

"Why am I not buying that?" he asked as he resumed cracking the eggs.

"You tell me, I'm not inside your head."

"So all of that you said last night, and you said a lot, that was all drunk-slash-blow-talk?"

Family Spirit

"And I had a couple hits off a fat joint."

"Damn, I gotta keep my eye on you, next party we're at."

"As opposed to the server from H. A. Winston's."

He concentrated on beating the eggs with a fork. "I'mma give that statement what it deserves, no response," he said. "Furthermore, I feel like you're just deflecting anyhow, 'cause, you know, the whole jealousy thing is hardly your style."

"Look, I admit that I have people in my family who are know-it-alls and claim that they can predict the future, but I was dressing it up last night, making it more than it was."

"That was some serious dressing up. So the whole ritual thing, is that for real, how does that work?"

"I told you, I was talking out of my head last night, I don't even remember what all I said." She popped bread in the toaster oven and focused on setting the timer so she didn't have to look at him. And then she did look at him, in his gray and red Temple sweatshirt, his gray sweatpants, his bare feet. She thought about deflecting for real, saying breakfast could wait because she felt a different kind of hunger coming on. He was so easy to distract that way. But the thought of it backfired on her, made her hungry for him. When did this happen? When did her desire to be with him reduce her to this swooning girl, the type she and Lynn and Charise would shake their head about, call pitiful, because she'd gone all in for a man to the detriment of herself?

"Well, what about the men, that was an exaggeration, too? The whole thing about the men being brought into the fold, is that for real?" he asked as he poured the eggs over the butter melting in the skillet, then sprinkled shredded cheese over the eggs.

She hunched her shoulders and looked at the toast browning in the oven.

"Because I'm all in, if that's the case. You know, and I pledged hard for my frat, and I said I'd never do no shit like that again. But I'd do it even harder for all the old heads in your family if it means I get to be with you. I swear to God, Lil. I'm in."

She winced then as she reached for the hot sheet pan to retrieve the toast without an oven mitt. Then she hollered, "Shit!" He turned on the cold water and grabbed for her hand to put it under the running water. "That was so stupid of me," she said. "God, how could I have been so stupid." She was talking about much more than reaching barehanded for the hot pan. And already blisters were forming on her fingers and forming inside her where the cold water could never reach.

✢ ✢ ✢

As difficult as it was trying to avoid Kevin's questions about her family—and when she couldn't, downplaying it all—it was harder being home. She found herself overcompensating by anticipating what GG needed and then rushing to do it before even being asked. She'd join GG on the porch to watch the sun set, and lean her head on GG's shoulder as she listened to her hum "How Great Thou Art." To give Bev a break, she'd bathe Miles and put him to bed, even when it wasn't her turn.

She'd do extra cleaning up after Pig, extra cooking, helped her mother with the books. And after all of that, she'd cry herself to sleep.

A week after she'd violated her family's sacred trust by talking about their gift outside of their established parameters, and by breathing Luda's name out loud, she received a call from *The Mike Douglas Show* to schedule an interview for the internship. Her elation after that phone call soothed just a little the cavernous places, the deeply dug wounds re-infected over and over from her constant rumination, her guilt.

So she was back in Wanamaker's basement, this time not to share a milkshake with Kevin. This time she was shopping for something to wear to the interview, with help from Lynn and Charise.

They were chattering away, excited for Lil, though protective, too. Lynn, the more serious of the two, asked Lil if she thought it odd that suddenly the people from *Mike Douglas* had called for an interview after she agreed to go all the way to Ohio with Kevin to meet his mom. "Sounds like some quid pro quo to me, and that's not cool."

But Charise said it was likely a coincidence. And Lynn said Lil should have someone look over the terms of the arrangement, and Charise countered that Lil was just an intern, boilerplate stuff for sure. Though they both wanted to know if she'd told her grandmother.

"Hell no, not yet."

"She might have some good advice," Lynn said.

"I want to surprise them all. So mum's the word."

They zipped their lips in unison, something else they'd being doing since they were very young, and then they commenced to swipe hangers to get Lil ready for her big debut. Navy suit, they agreed, with shoulder pads, so she could be properly dressed to rub elbows with the big boys.

13.

Stars

The greenroom was hardly green save for the lettuce garnishing the fruit bowl. It was more yellow; at least that's what Lil noticed. The yellow had escaped her the times she'd been in here since landing the internship, delivering some necessity to a guest, like Excedrin, or a safety pin, or real cream instead of the nondairy variety set up near the coffee carafes. Today she was the guest, and there was a bunch of bananas holding down the center of the table, the table spread with finger sandwiches and crudites. She thought the bananas odd. For one, it was the afternoon and bananas seemed like a breakfast fruit, and otherwise, who would take time to peel a banana and bite it in sections before going on live television. Then there was the banana peel. Ugh, she thought. She was allergic to bananas, and she felt a wave of nausea trying to overtake her because that was all she could smell once she looked at them, and she guessed that was why she was seeing yellow everywhere.

There were four televisions, one on each wall, broadcasting the show. Mike Douglas was interviewing a blond author in a tan suit and yellow blouse. Her smile was too wide, exposing all of her gums and excessive overbite. Lil made a mental note to mitigate her own smile, which gushed freely. She was glad that Lynn and Charise had talked her into wearing the same outfit she'd worn to the interview that had landed her the internship. Navy suit with a crisp sky-blue shirt, a perfectly folded three-point pocket square of fuchsia, purple, and white saluting from the breast pocket. Her hair, still straightened, was pressed back in a ponytail held intact by a wide barrette so that she could fan the ponytail in the back. Lynn had come over earlier, and they'd gone into the dressing room to do her hair and makeup, as Lynn had insisted that a white makeup person would have her looking like Morticia from *The Addams Family*.

Lil took deep breaths. She was nervous. Told herself it was okay to be nervous after the whirlwind couple of weeks she'd had, from the interview to what was about to happen now, her actual appearance on set with Michael Douglas to do a promo for the "What Is Hip" segment, which they'd changed to "What Is Cool," and added three other interns to also conduct interviews on the street, white girls, and when Lil asked Kevin why, he'd said, "'Cause this is America, baby, you know that's how the shit works."

Kevin had already breezed through the greenroom three times. "You need anything? You comfortable? Any questions?" He was more nervous than she was, she could tell by the way he kept biting his lower lip. She'd never noticed him doing that until the past couple of weeks, when she'd see him at work, always in passing because they knew to keep a professional distance from each other. Several times she'd try to wink at him when no one else was around, and he'd bite his lower lip and look away. And later, when they were together after that first day, after he'd shed his navy blue blazer and his work face, he apologized for acting like a tin man. She'd told him don't dare insult the Tin Man, the Tin Man was her favorite character in *The Wiz*.

"I can't let my guard down a little bit around there. I wink back at you, next thing I'm gonna forget where I am and start putting my hands all over you." She knew that was an exaggeration. From what she'd gleaned of his work behavior, there was no forgetting where he was when he was there, no letting his guard down. Even when he apologized, his jaw was clenched, and she jokingly asked if she needed to slide a little oil to him. Then he loosened up and let out a real laugh, not the forced imitation laughs she'd overhear when he was with his colleagues.

Now in the greenroom, he could talk to her because this was part of his job, a big part, she learned, to keep the guests comfortable. The superstars could be demanding, but the ones still climbing were the worst, showing up with their agents and publicists and dogs. Kevin's immediate supervisor had asked Lil to walk a quasi-star's dog. She'd just finished for the day and was on her way to leave the building to get to her afternoon class. "Oh, I'd love to," she'd said, pulling out her disarming smile. "But the professor of the class I'm headed to is a stickler for time and closes the door ten minutes after the start of class, so if I'm not in my seat, I'm absent. But I'm sure if you call the liaison of the intern program, they'll be happy to intercede on my behalf, because the contract I signed stipulates that class attendance takes priority over any—" He'd raised his hand to stop her and moved quickly down the hall.

She'd told Kevin how she'd gotten out of walking the little bitch, and he'd laughed at first, then bitten his lip again and said, "You know I would have been happy to call the liaison and work things out for you."

"I didn't want it worked out," she'd said, irritated with him for seeming to take the company's side over her own. "I wanted to get to my class on time."

"No, I hear you, babe," he said. "But being at the station is a huge opportunity for you."

"Got that. But me being there is a bit of an opportunity for them, too. My grandmom always told us we bring something good to and take something good from every situation if we let our light shine." She'd referenced GG a lot to him after the night she'd bled the sacred story of her family's powers all over his apartment. She was still bleeding the guilt of it, which caused her to invoke her grandmother's wisdom to compensate, because she blamed him, too.

She looked at Kevin now. His lower lip was so red and swollen that she was about to ask him who punched him in the mouth. But before she could, he said, "Let's go," as he motioned her to stand. "Your time to shine, Ms. Mace."

"Let's do it," she said, standing straight and tall, ignoring the centrifugal bananas that had tried so hard to make her sick, ignoring the television. She wanted to ignore Kevin, too, but he was pulling her arm. She turned to look at him. "What?"

He put his hands on her arms and rubbed them up and down. "I just want to say, I want to say—" He was stammering. "Kevin, what?" she said, trying to hurry him along.

His forehead had a sheen of sweat, and he was biting his lip; so hard she thought any moment his lip would squirt blood all over her navy suit that she'd had dry-cleaned, though she'd worn it only once, her meticulously ironed shirt. His eyes went soupy, as if he were about to cry. "Are you okay?" she asked, thinking, What the fuck.

"I just want to say that I love you, I really do. I love you, Lillianna Mace."

She didn't say she loved him back. Did she even love him back? Or—now that she was so close she could taste it—did she really only love what he could do for her. She didn't even know how to admit that to herself, so she didn't. She put her hand to her mouth and blew him a kiss, then turned quickly toward the door that led to the set. She focused on the door as she floated more than walked toward it, going higher, a rising star. That's what he was calling her these days. His rising star. "You know that stars are most visible after night falls," she'd said the last time he called her that. They were at his apartment, and she'd said it with a salacious wink, and he was all over then, calling her his night star.

She knew that the two were inextricably linked, her star rising, her night falling, as she sauntered through that door onto the set, the set paradoxically ablaze with so many lights.

She settled herself on the couch adjacent to Mike Douglas's desk as his makeup person swiped his forehead and nose with powder, and his producer walked through saying, "Forty-five seconds!," and she breathed in deeply, pulling the breath all the way into her stomach, preparing for the darkness that would soon surround her.

The vision she'd had on the bus after she'd first met Kevin and gone back to his bare apartment and kissed his bare chest and bared herself the way she never had, the vision that had made her cry out no, no, no, the entire bus ride home: that vision was that the Mace family home built by GG's father would explode. She'd heard the sound first and then the sight of it. The center of the house pushed up from below ground, pulling the substance with it, the brick and mortar of it, the glass and wood, all converging into energy and then smoke and then ash. She realized now that what she'd seen was not the house exploding but a metaphor for a different type of explosion. Hearts, a family being blown apart.

14.

Show Time

Lil waited for the signal that the commercial would end in ten seconds and they'd go live. She counted down in her head. She was sure that every Mace was watching: She'd asked Bev to alert the family to tune in because she might get a mention on air; she wanted to surprise them that it was not only a mention, they'd actually see her sitting there chatting it up with Mike Douglas.

He introduced her and said that the "What Is Cool" segment had been the brainchild of a cadre of talented interns like her, and the show was fortunate to have them all on board. He asked what her favorite part was about working on the segment, and she replied, "Every person has a story that only they have lived, that only they can tell, and I feel really privileged to have the opportunity to give voice to those stories that put our shared humanity on display. And it helps that the stories we will be elevating, as the title of the segment suggests, are really pretty cool." She raised and lowered her brows as if a conductor were in front of her with a baton, guiding her to move her eyes, tilt her head, her leans forward and backward to match the rhythm of her words, to reinforce the ideas she expressed; she even remembered to contain her smile. She was making music as she spoke. When she finished, the audience clapped without waiting for the applause sign to flash.

And now the vision she'd had on the bus that had made her moan no, no, no was so close to its outworking that she thought she could hear it rumbling like the beast in a horror film, just outside of view, as if it were in the greenroom sitting next to Kevin, who was watching on the four televisions back there, going from one screen to the next because he couldn't bear to keep his eyes on the same screen for any length of time. Fitting that she'd experienced the Knowing right after she'd left him the day they'd met. They'd be forever linked, her star rising, her night falling, her house exploding, Kevin.

"Speaking of cool," Mike Douglas said once the applause ended, "I understand that you've got one of the coolest stories I've heard lately. I understand that you have inherited a gene from your ancestor Lydia that's given you superpowers and you can see into the future."

Lil wondered if she'd misheard, if her desperate want for this man not to give voice to the sacred name of Luda, on live television no less, had scrambled the signals traveling to her auditory cortex. No, she was sure, he'd said Lydia. At least he'd said Lydia.

Still, she could feel the reverberation all the way from

Southwest Philly to this small space that was the set of *The Mike Douglas Show*. Considering the impact on her in this moment, she thought the set should be so much larger, larger than the Civic Center, where she and her mother and GG and Bev would walk its width and length to take in every bloom at the Flower Show, larger than the Spectrum, where her father had taken them to see Dr. J fly through the air, larger even than the Roman Colosseum, which had cheered on the destruction of life, the way she was being cheered on in the midst of her life's destruction.

Surely at this moment, her mother was staring blankly in shock as if witnessing her child being hit by a bus, and Bev was muttering in a sudsy voice as she held back tears, *What the ever-loving fuck have you done, Lil*. And her grandmother, Lil's heart ached for her grandmother, the keeper of their culture, didn't she know? Lil wondered. Surely she must have known how large Lil's wanting was for other things, for the world outside their home lovingly encased under Luda's rainbow. Surely that was why she was so intent on preparing Lil to replace her, in the hope that she could short-circuit Lil's outsize wanting, redirect it back to their practice, their home. And since GG had known, she had to have knelt on the side of her bed, the way she did every night after she'd turned down her white-ribbed bedspread, and white satin-edged blanket, and white cotton top sheet, and prayed. Lil thought now that was why Mike Douglas had just mispronounced Luda's name, an act of God, her grandmother's intercessory prayer to keep her infraction from being far worse.

"So, I have a crystal ball here," Mike Douglas continued. "And I'd like to know what you see for me in the future."

Lil didn't miss a beat as she angled her body away from the crystal ball. Her family would never be associated with such a gimmick, such a debasement of who they were, as if they were some corner store–dwelling two-bit fortune tellers, as if they'd not been ordained by God and the ancestors to chart a single thread in the tapestry of a person's life that moved them into tomorrow, today. She could at least disavow the crystal ball, even though she'd violated a sacred trust and spoken of Luda to an outsider; she could at least not reduce herself to validating such an offensive prop.

She flashed her widened eyes and tilted her head and said, "Actually, Mr. Douglas, I have never used a crystal ball, and certainly I don't need one now to tell you what I see coming very soon for you." She invoked a dramatic pause and looked into the camera and pursed her lips in a playful smile and moved her eyes back and forth between the camera and the studio audience. She could sense the audience holding their breath in anticipation. "I see a commercial break in your future."

The studio audience howled. Even Mike Douglas laughed and, experienced host that he was, knew how to end an interview on a high note. "Ladies and gentlemen, another hand for our star intern, Lillianna Mace."

Lil smiled and nodded to the applause and turned to Mike Douglas, acknowledging him. They cut to a break. "That was fantastic," he said. The makeup person rushed to him to dust his nose. His head producer was in his ear, prepping him for the next segment. Lil walked off the set, walked through a greenroom that seemed darker. No Kevin anywhere, just the bananas, now showing brown spots, just the lettuce adorning the fruit, now wilted, just a human heart exploded, drifting back down to cover the speckled carpet, tattered, seemingly beyond repair.

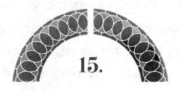

15.

Miss Lady

Lil had nowhere to go but home. She was remarkably calm on the trolley headed up Woodland Avenue. She wondered if she was in shock, or if she was experiencing some type of inappropriate-affect mental breakdown. Even her thoughts of Kevin were charitable. She'd told him, willingly, sacred things. Surely a part of her had known that this would be the result. Separation. A break as sure and exacting as a sharpened cleaver taking one good hack to the wing joint of a just-thawed Christmas turkey. A clean cut as soon as Mike Douglas had said Luda's name, mispronounced though it was. She'd thought that Mike Douglas saying Lydia instead of Luda was a result of her grandmother's prayers. Though as she considered it on the trolley ride, perhaps Kevin had intentionally spoken the wrong name, making himself at least a candidate for redemption.

By the time she walked toward her already-once-home,

there was Bev out front. Bev's eyes were red. Her face was puffy. Lil thought that Bev was holding her most difficult emotion in her face. She understood the cacophony of feelings rankling Bev right now. Lil walked toward the feelings, the anger and sorrow, the regret, the disappointment. She walked into the feelings. She was intent on sharing them with Bev the way they'd shared everything to make things manageable: They'd shared tending to Miles; bearing the weight of their chronically fatigued mother; the constant wishing that GG had at least one other daughter so that Lil and Bev could have enjoyed first cousins who would have been as close to them as sisters and needed allies when the day came and they'd have to battle with Helene's line of carping offspring who envied them because they were nearest to the family's seat of power; they'd shared the perpetual hoping that their father would stay put this time, the next time, the time after that, which never came because he was always leaving, not staying; they'd shared the frustration over Helene's intent to keep a fight smoldering, always poking the ashes and looking for the hidden coals causing them to erupt. And then there was GG. They'd shared their devotion to GG, their awe of her, their conflictions, too, because she asked for as much as she gave, but she gave so much that her askings were large, certainly too large for Lil. Lil knew that Bev understood that for everything the sisters had shared as equally as they could, there was no equal distribution between them for what GG expected of Lil.

So Lil and Bev embraced outside the house. It was a long and close embrace, so close that they could hear the clinking sounds in the other's heart as the shattered pieces separated and fell away.

There were no words, none to speak or sigh. Just gestures as Lil looked up at the house and Bev put a hand on her face to redirect her. She shook her head ferociously. No goodbyes to their mother, to dearest Miles, to lovely Pig, to GG.

Bev handed Lil the bag she'd packed for her, then turned and walked back up the steps, leaving Lil standing on the sidewalk, under the tree with the massive roots that were growing into the basement, the foundation of the house. Lil thought she could hear offshoots of the roots making tiny fissures through the basement floor, even while the pavement was beginning to crack as the tree pushed upward, too. She pushed upward then, and down deep, too, as she started walking, and after about a mile and a half, her black leather pumps rubbing against her heels, she was at the corner that housed the bar and the church. She went into the bar. She sat down next to a man who could be her father's age. "You running away from home, Miss Lady?" he asked her.

"Home's running away from me," she said.

"What you drinking, sweetheart?"

"Whatever you are."

"Yo, give this young lady a gin and tonic and hold the gin," he said to the barmaid.

"I should have gone across the street into the church," she said, and smirked. "At least I could have hunted down their stash of Communion wine."

"You don't need no wine, Miss Lady, you just need to dance."

He pulled her up to the familiar square of a dance floor where the ghost of a woman had pulled her weeks ago. Michael Jackson's voice poured down from the speakers overhead. He was singing "I'll Be There." The man held her loosely around the waist and led her in a two-step. She'd never followed men well on slow songs, but she did then. It felt like a miracle as she allowed him to twirl her around: She was right on cue with the dip. Then he pulled her in close and sang in her ear the part of the song that said: *Just call my name and I'll be there.* She rested her head on his shoulder then and started to cry. He held her and swayed with her until she stopped. "You know I love you," he said in a voice that was unrecognizable because it was so different from the voice he'd used otherwise. She wondered whose voice it was. Not her father's, not Kevin's. Must have been God's, she thought as he escorted her back to her seat at the bar where her bag rested and her virgin gin and tonic waited.

She went back to Kevin's later that night. She had nowhere else to go. He opened the door and looked at her as if she were a mirage, as if he were walking through a desert, parched, close to death, and there was a freshwater lake that he could drink from to save his own life.

He babbled out an apology in stammered sobs. He only told his boy Sam, he swore. Lil liked Sam, the only other black person on the production team; he had an honest smile and a backbone.

"He was telling me about some potent blow he'd had over the weekend," Kevin said, rushing his words, "how the shit had made him damn near hallucinate, and I told him the same thing happened to you, how you started talking about being from a clairvoyant family, how you could see into the future. And I saw his eyes light up, and I played it down, I swear to you I did. But then Sam crafted a whole idea for a skit where you'd tell fortunes of people in the studio audience. He didn't tell me he was going to do that shit, I swear. And when I found out, I was like, 'Hell no, that's my lady's personal shit, no.' But he'd already run with it. You know, they've been pressuring everybody about ratings and shit. But I fought hard to kill it; you don't know how hard I fought to kill it. I did manage to get it pared down to what it was, just the one question from Mike. And you aced it, I knew you would. God, I knew you would."

They stood there looking at each other, two feet apart. He knew not to get closer, not to try to touch her, hug her. He was smart in that way. The radiator made clanking sounds, reminding her how warm it was, unseasonably warm, and she still had on her coat, was still carrying the bag Bev had packed for her so she knew she would have what she needed for the short term. She still had on her pumps that she'd walked in all the way here from the bar. She'd walked miles in those pumps today, walked into her future in those pumps. And her aunt Helene would be proud because she was wearing a lightweight panty girdle. She was tired. She was hot. She was filled with tonic water sans the gin, and she had to pee.

She let her bag fall from where her hand had surrounded

the straps. It thudded onto the circle rug filled with orange and yellow swirls; she'd given him the rug to add some color to the room so the room wouldn't sync up with the monotones of nothingness she'd seen that morning during the ritual.

"I need someplace to stay," she said, her voice with no color, just a one-note intended to give him nothing.

He managed to extract hope still as he exclaimed, "Oh God, Lil, you know you can stay here, God yes, for as long as you need, forever."

"Not forever," she said. "Just until I no longer need." She shook her coat from her shoulders and went into the bathroom to relieve herself.

✦ ✦ ✦

Lil and Kevin became roommates. He took the couch, she the bed. They split the cost of groceries. She would have halved the rent with him, too, but her internship didn't pay that much. She almost lost the internship because she'd performed so well with the crystal-ball segment that they wanted to make it regular. Kevin suggested that she go to human resources and tell them that she would work on the planning of the segment but would not participate on air because it would infringe on her religious beliefs. All talk of the segment halted, as did any comments about her supposed clairvoyance. She assumed Kevin had worked behind the scenes on her behalf, but she still drew a line that kept him out.

They had civil conversations about work, politics, a movie they'd seen, a book they'd read, an eccentric neighbor always leaving bowls of cooked lima beans up and down the block. They didn't talk about feelings, though; they didn't talk about thoughts that went beyond the waxy surface. She sometimes went to parties with him, though she declined to go to Ohio to meet his mother. She took advantage of his absence and hosted a Christmas brunch. Lynn and Charise, Bev and her dad and Miles, all came brimming with gifts and laughter and stories. She cried when it was time for them to leave, so Bev and Miles spent the night. Sensible Bev had an overnight bag in the trunk.

Lil matured in the months she lived with Kevin. She was more introspective, she laughed less, talked less, she grew new skin, smooth but thicker. Missing GG and her mother still hurt, though, sometimes with a pang that made her breath stop, other times a dull ache; mostly it was the sense of the sagging emptiness they once filled that was the worst.

16.

Elevation

Bev and their dad threw Lil a graduation diner at Moshulu on Penn's Landing. She'd graduated with honors after all. They brought Miles with them, and invited Lynn and Charise, and Vivian, who cleaned the bathrooms at the television station, and the interns Lil worked with.

When Lil was leaving for the party in her white eyelet sundress and three-inch espadrille sandals, Kevin, in white pants and blue linen shirt with a white skinny tie, joked with Lil that he was all dressed up and had nowhere to go.

"So find somewhere to go," she said as she pushed the hat over her crinkly hair and pulled her sunglasses from her purse.

"I was hoping I could get a last-minute invite to the gig your sis and pops are throwing for you."

She put her shades on and turned to look at him directly. "If you're ready for my sister to kick your ass, sure, you can come. But she's a fighter, and I guarantee you she will take you down."

"So we'll never get past this," he said.

She hunched her shoulders. She was glad she had the sunglasses on so he wouldn't see her eyes water. "No feelings talk, remember the rule."

"That was your rule."

"And it still stands," she said, opening the door to the hallway crowded with bikes, and then the main door that led out to Juniper Street, all leafed out under a brilliant midday sun.

"Did you ever even love me at all?" he called behind her as she walked down the steps. "Because I really loved you, and I still do. You hear me, Lil? I still do." He kept repeating it. His voice followed her down the block. She could hear the suds in his voice. The neighbor who left bowls of covered lima beans on random people's steps was doing her thing. She looked up at Lil, then looked down the street at Kevin yelling that he still loved her. She shook her head as she resumed setting out the bowls containing the limas. "Crazy people in this world," she said.

Lil's dad had invited one of his colleagues, Jennifer, a woman in her sixties with a pale brown complexion and silver hair and white thick-soled comfort shoes. Lil liked her. She reminded her of GG if GG were sweeter. She was an analyst, like her dad, for the Department of Labor. She offered to spread Lil's résumé around, said that her sister had an influential position with a media conglomerate. "In fact, please give my sister a call," she said, as if it were an afterthought, though she had her sister's business card at the ready and handed it to Lil. "She saw your segment on *Mike Douglas*, and I told her I work with your dad, and she asked me to please get her number to you. She has a sense of your capabilities and would love to chat with you."

"I certainly shall," Lil said. "Can you let her know to expect to hear from me?"

She nodded. Lil caught her father's expression from the corner of her eye. He nodded, too, pleased.

Her name was Lydia, the same name that Mike Douglas had used when he'd mispronounced Luda's name. Lydia mentioned that immediately the day Lil took the train into New York and walked to Lydia's office in midtown and rode the elevator straight up to heaven, that's how high the floor number was. The elevator didn't stop from the ground floor to the top, though Lil's stomach got off midway, so she was woozy when they ushered her back to Lydia's voluminous office with walls that also stretched up, and up some more to accommodate the art and the power. Lil wondered how Lydia kept from feeling small with the excessive height of objects surrounding her until Lydia came from behind her desk to shake Lil's hand, and Lil saw that her stature was elevated, too, with her stilettos and big hair and big shoulder pads on her red power-suit jacket that fell neatly over the pencil skirt hiding her hips but not the idea of them.

As they walked the block to get to the couch on the other side of the room, Lydia said, "My big sister loves your dad, calls him her surrogate baby brother." By the time they were seated, Lydia was already into the story of how she had her television on as background noise the day Lil appeared on *Mike Douglas*. "I only looked up when I heard him say my name. Call me odd or not, depending on your leaning, but I believe the universe sends us messages, and Mike Douglas calling my name was the universe saying, 'Pay attention, lady.' And I did. You were so striking, Lil, so poised, it was hard to believe you were just an intern. And you totally handled Mike Douglas with the whole crystal-ball shtick. I called my sister and said that you were the real deal. I could see it in your eyes. I see it now."

Lil didn't say thank you. She sensed that Lydia wasn't trying to compliment her; she was stating what she thought was a fact. Lil nodded and said that she found the crystal ball a tad gimmicky.

"Why so?"

"If someone can really see into the future, they likely won't use a crystal ball."

"So can you?"

"Can I what?"

"See into the future? Mike Douglas said you could."

"He also wanted me to use a crystal ball."

"Yep, yep, yep. I knew it," she said. "I knew you'd be this sharp. Would you like to come work for me?"

Lil had thought this would be a scratch-and-sniff, not a job offer. She had GG's voice in her head, saying, "When you're blindsided and have to make a response, don't act shocked, just pause. Let the response come to you, don't let your mind go running around frantically trying to find the response. It will come to you if you pause for the count of three and allow it to come."

So Lil paused for just a few seconds, straight-backed, face in neutral, and it came to her, and she asked calmly, "In what capacity would I be working for you?"

"As my special assistant."

"And I'd be responsible for?"

"To be direct, Lil, because I sense you can handle directness, I need a seer. As you can imagine, a Black woman in this office with its wraparound views takes incoming from all sides. So I'm dealing with blind spots out the wazoo. Essentially, I need someone who can ride shotgun and let me know when I can change lanes. I need your eyes, Lil. That's what I need. And I'm willing to pay."

Lil paused again. She wanted to say that her eyes were not for sale. Her communications skills, her ability to target message, to construct an inverted pyramid in her sleep, to draft a feature on paint drying that sparkled with intrigue: Those skills were negotiable, but not her eyes. Her eyes were her calling. And yet she'd sat on the porch with her grandmother countless mornings as the sun asked the night to move over, to give it room to shine, and she'd watched her grandmother negotiate the Maces' eyes. Whether for money or for services worth more than money, GG put a price tag on their eyes, often much lower than GG's sisters or their offspring would have liked, but a price tag nonetheless. It was coming to her now that her grandmother believed their gift of sight was ordained by God and the ancestors, and that the people who found their way to them by someone they trusted whispering in their ear "I know a woman" had been sent to them by God, so GG was merely following the natural ebb and flow of giving according to one's talents and receiving according to one's needs.

"I can't commit to being a psychic on demand," Lil said as she wondered who'd whispered in Lydia's ear that they knew a woman.

"Oh, I do understand that. I'm not Mike Douglas. No crystal ball required," Lydia said, smiling so wide she showed all her gums. Lil thought she had a smile like her mother's when Hortense could muster the energy it took to fix her face in a smile.

They talked logistics then, a breathtaking salary offer by Lil's standards—she was earning pennies an hour during her internship—relocation, even temporary housing in a company-owned loft until she secured an apartment.

Lil confessed to Lydia that she was ready to say yes, but she'd be more comfortable giving it some thought and talking it through with her family: "As the old folks say, I need to pray on this." They both laughed then from deep places.

When they were standing as face-to-face as they could, given that Lydia had at least four inches on Lil, Lil asked if she'd ever met Thad, her father. "No, but I'd love to," Lydia said. "If you accept our offer and move here, your parents can visit, and we can all get acquainted."

Family Spirit

They shook hands, and Lil walked to the elevator thinking how genuine Lydia was, how authentic, how she'd love to work with her, despite the fact that in the split second right after she'd asked Lydia if she'd met her father, the sun that was cutting through the tall windows took Lydia's face in its hands, held her at the perfect angle for Lil to see the barely perceptible squint to her eyes, the way her lower and upper jaw moved away from each other, pushing her lips closer, to an I-have-a-secret closeness, and in the next split of a second, her face had reopened in a smile, and she'd said, "No, but I'd love to."

Lil didn't visibly cry when she said her goodbyes. Nor did Bev, who'd always considered herself too mean and unsentimental. Though Bev did arrange to take Pig to the park without GG so that Bev and Lil and their beloved Pig could spend some time. Her father was too elated to cry; in fact it was difficult for him to suppress his giddiness that his daughter was actually moving to the Big Apple to work for one of the most powerful Black women in media, and giddy for other reasons as well, Lil knew. Lynn and Charise were excited for Lil and for themselves, because with Lil in New York, their shopping and clubbing landscapes were expanding exponentially.

And Kevin, Kevin did cry. The night before Lil's departure, she relaxed her no-feelings rule and let him in, let him handle her in places that had softened for him finally. And they climbed the tree together to the top, where the night sky met the branches, and they held on to the sky and each other. When she woke the next morning, he was gone. He left her a note on his side of the bed: *It's gonna hurt too much to watch you leave.* In the living room was an oversize box, wrapped and bowed in Christmas paper that made her smile, because he always complained that whenever he had to wrap a gift in the summer, all he ever had around was Christmas paper. She tore the paper off gingerly so she could fold it up and put it in a bag and write on the bag, *To use for the next gift you have to wrap in the summer.*

She opened the box. There was a meticulously folded peacoat, hip-length, double-breasted, just like the one she'd bought that day when they first met. But better. Not from I Goldberg but from a designer she'd never heard of because their brand never ended up in Wanamaker's basement. The wool was richer, the navy deeper. The sentiment left fingerprints on her heart. The note inside said, *Yes, I really did want to pay for it.*

She tried to convince herself she wasn't crying, even as she watched the thirsty coat swallow up her tears.

The Little Drummer Boy

December 2019, Nona Philly-bound

Christmas fell on a Sunday, so Nona and Bob planned to go to church in Philly because Nona was anxious to get to her cousins' and dole out the gifts to their grandchildren. She loved Christmas with them, the way they'd spread around the oversize dining table made even larger with the leaves. The food was substantial and substantially good. The talk was loud like the jokes, and even the arguments were fun. No one followed the talk-then-listen rule; it was talk when you can get in, listen only if you must. Nona loved it all.

"You think you have enough presents here?" Bob asked as they loaded the SUV. At first Nona thought he was joking, so she laughed, but he didn't laugh; his too-tanned skin from his latest, longest layover in the sands of Maui tightened around his jawline, letting her know he wasn't in the mood for laughter. So she let him have this funky mood he was in, even as she realized she'd been doing that a lot lately. "And are we going to need an armed guard to watch the car while we're in the church? Because who knows how far away we'll have to park."

"We could drop the gifts at Sissy's first," she said, buckling herself in.

"And where are we even going to park around her house?"

"We'll find parking."

"You have the address loaded in the GPS?"

"I know how to get there."

"Yeah, but your way will take us through the nooks and crannies and alleys."

"I promise, no alleys. This tanker couldn't get through an alley, anyway."

"Could you just load the address in the GPS, please? It will keep us on the main routes. And I'd rather stick to the main routes."

"I'd rather take the shortcuts," she said as she pulled down the mirror to check her lipstick; her lips were unusually dry.

"Okay, we get carjacked at a red light in some alleyway, remember we went your route."

"Okay, but odds are better we get shot closer to home by some assault-weapon-carrying white nationalist who looks at your red skin and swears you're an immigrant coming for his job as a pizza delivery man."

"My skin isn't that red."

"It is after your last layover. You was getting some mucho sun, babe."

He didn't say anything. She wished he would say something, defend himself. "So am I right?" she pushed.

"About what?"

"About you sunning it up on your damn near three-day layover."

"I'm not going to argue," he said. "There'll be enough arguing going down at your cousins."

The car was quiet then, save the sound of the tension between them buzzing like flies in and out of her ears. She sang silently to herself to shut the buzzing down; she sang the song the Mace women sang during their rituals to help a seer along.

> *Pour back into us your peace that we let go, the gift,*
>   *the glorious gift,*
> *calm us with your glow, from head to heart to soul, to*
>   *make us whole,*
> *that we may know. The gift, the glorious gift.*
> *Oh, sweet, sweet Spirit, calm us with your glow,*
> *that we may know. That we may know.*

She sang it in her head all the way to Philly while Bob listened to some preacher on Sirius. And then she did know.

Once they got in to the part of the city where Bob grew uncomfortable, Nona insisted on driving. She took the smallest streets she could think of so his discomfort would blossom. She regretted that they weren't in South Philly. Alleys galore in South Philly.

She softened by the time they got to the church service. An adorable children's choir sang "Little Drummer Boy," and a boy about three years old stood front and center on the rostrum, not singing but making all kinds of hilarious gestures, from using his cupped hands as a telescope and panning the congregation, to thumbing his lips, to moving his hands as if playing a piano. Nona thought of a young Miles as she watched him. The congregation worked to restrain their laughter. Bob took her hand and squeezed it. She moved in closer to him so that their shoulders touched. His shoulders were shaking. "Too funny, right?" she leaned in and whispered. And when she did, she saw rivers pouring down his face. Her first thought was that he was taking "laughing till you cry" to the next level; her second thought was of Hackensack, New Jersey. She'd used Hackensack as she wrote the scene detailing scenarios when a person might seek out the Maces, such as a woman who might be wondering if her husband had a whole 'nother family in Hackensack. She thought Hackensack so clever, the name of the place so appropriate for a cheating spouse to have a whole family on the side.

Her third thought was that she'd delete that Hackensack line from the story because the story no longer needed it. The story already knew. It had always been up to her to discover it for herself.

She took her hand from his. She reached into her purse and pulled out a tissue and dropped it on his lap. She began singing in her head again, the line from the Mace song. *That we may know. That we may know. That we may know.*

17.

Philly

2019

Lil nestled into the butter-soft couch and took in the smell of new leather. It was after midnight and quiet in the family room Lorna had designed, which could be on the cover of *House Beautiful* with its grays and blues and pops of orange and red, its symmetry of couch facing couch, swivel club chairs slightly askance to allow for turning into, or away from, conversation. She'd seen the room in earlier iterations when Miles had texted her pictures telling her this room would be the opening image on Lorna's website when she launched her interior design business. Lil had replied with heart emojis. She knew that he constantly updated her because she'd given them seed money for the venture. She didn't want him to feel indebted. Had insisted to him every time he came to her for money, "What's mine is thine, baby brother."

She certainly had it to spare. After Lydia introduced her to well-placed agent friends in the publishing and entertainment worlds, Lil went on to pen a series of bestselling how-to books about harnessing the power of intuition; she became a headliner at conferences and a media darling/frequent guest on morning talk shows. And then there was what she considered her best work: when someone came to her referred by a person in whom they confided, who'd simply said, "I know a woman."

She sank deeper into the couch, glad that she'd asked Miles if she could stay with them while she underwent a medical procedure: It would give him the opportunity to feel he was doing something for her for a change. Though he'd never know how much he'd done just by being Miles, lovable, thoughtful, wide-smiling Miles.

She texted with Bev now, telling her what a good time she was having with baby brother and his family. *They got their drama for sure, but mad humor, too*, she wrote. *With Lorna trying to get her interior design business up and running, while Miles is all immersed in his novel and going crazy trying to get a book deal. And then there's this big-butt neighbor of theirs who's always walking her black dog, always pausing in front of this house, and Miles—God love his sometimes too-friendly self—goes running outside, his smile so wide I think it's gonna get caught in his earlobes, and stands out there grinning and chatting with the chile. But yesterday I guess Lorna had had enough so she went out there and called Miles in, and the dog jumps up on Miles as if telling him to stay, and the woman laughs and looks up at Lorna and plasters a fake innocent smile on her face and says to Lorna, This dog sure does love Miles, and Lorna says, So I notice, all the black bitches around here seem to love him.*

Lil went on to text how she'd laughed so hard she'd almost peed on herself. She laughed now, a deep laugh, a necessary laugh after her appointment earlier with the oncologist, who'd confirmed what the doctors had told her, the lesion on her liver was in fact a hepatocellular carcinoma. The good news was that it was small, so small that she had so many options: a liver resection, where they'd carve off a third of her liver, and after a couple of months of recovery, she'd be back to living her good life; or targeted radiation, where they could hit the spot and zap the hell out of it; or microwave it into nothingness with ablation; or push a needle through her groin into her liver and drop a bolus of chemo right there, only there, to kill that sucker. Options, so many options.

She'd told only her New York agent about her diagnosis, and Bev, of course Bev. Her agent had suggested Sloan Kettering. "You've got to go to Sloan," she insisted. "Everybody who's anybody who knows goes to Sloan."

Bev said simply, "Come on home, Lil. Just come on home."

Lil told everyone else that it was a pesky upper abdominal cyst she had to deal with. She didn't like to say "liver cancer." No pink ribbons or Schuylkill River trail walks or foundations named for survivors of cancer that started in the liver, cancers that had not traveled from a more respectable place like the breast or the brain. Even she herself, as worldly and open-minded as she was, had always associated primary liver cancer with alcoholics, drug addicts, undernourished skid row dwellers. And though she'd maintained a relatively healthy lifestyle, she knew that her tumor was from hep C, which she'd been cured of, though she was one of the outliers who, despite the cure, still went on to have this type of lesion squirming around in her liver, trying to get comfortable so that it could thrive.

The hep C was surely caused by her casual cocaine use during the months she'd stayed with Kevin after the explosion that had separated her from her family. Kevin took her to the parties where they could indulge. She didn't blame him. She took full responsibility for the lines she'd snort at parties they'd attend, where she'd get high with strangers. She'd once noticed a drop of blood on the mirror she'd used. Was it hers? Was it from the messy-haired white boy who'd gone before her? It didn't matter. She needed all the substance that her nostrils could hold back then. Needed the substance to travel to her heart to fill in all the shattered places, to compensate for all the goodbyes she never got to say.

Her phone vibrated. Bev was texting her back a line of laughing-face emojis over the story she'd just told about Lorna and the big-butt woman with the dog. *A tale of two bitches*, Bev wrote. *Three if you count the dog*, followed by more laughing emojis.

Leave my girl Lorna alone, Lil replied.

I'm just saying if that woman was not my brother's wife and my niece's mother . . .

And taking such good care of your only sister, Lil texted. *I'm having a good time over here. They keep me laughing.*

Family Spirit

You win, Bev replied, *we'll put Lorna's bitch title on pause for now, 'cause I'm so glad you're there with them.*

Me too, me too, Lil texted, adding praying hands. She felt herself getting filled up and was about to allow herself to sob, but then she heard Ayana bouncing down the stairs, so she sat up and put on a happy face, and when Ayana said, "What's up, Aunt?," Lil was happy for real.

"You tell me, Booby."

"Well, we had a book signing at the café tonight and I stayed late to help. I felt compelled to, since I suggested that they use the space in the evenings. Bree came, and we hung out for a little after."

"Bree's good?"

"She's the best. I know Aunt Bev isn't into her mom, and I guess it's mutual for Aunt Carlotta, but Bree is my total ride-or-die."

"See, so there can be peace on earth, just leave it to the next generation. And who was signing books?"

"A local writer, just calls herself Miss. She did a graphic novel about a pig. Totally into pigs, too. She had on a sweatshirt silk-screened with a pig, pig earrings, a pig tattoo."

"I totally get the pig obsession. Your daddy ever tell you about Pig?"

"Ever tell me?" Ayana said, shaping her face in exaggerated pain. "If we pass a farm and see a pig, or watch a commercial that has a pig in it, or if Dad's reading a magazine and there's a picture of a pig, he'll get all misty and say, 'That looks just like Pig.' And I'm thinking, Duh, well, what pig wouldn't look just like Pig. Then he'll have the nerve to ask, 'Did I ever tell you about Pig?' And both Mom and I will yell, 'Yes!' Because if he gets started on Pig, that's an hour, at least."

Lil laughed, even as she got an unexpected pang of missing Pig all over again.

"Can I ask you something, Aunt Lil?" Ayana said as she plopped in the swivel chair and angled it toward Lil.

"Anything."

"Probably not supposed to ask you this, but why didn't you have children?"

Lil covered her face with her hands and made sobbing sounds. Ayana jumped from the chair and in one move was at the couch, hovering over Lil, saying, "Oh my God, Aunt, I'm sorry, that was such an insensitive question. I knew I shouldn't have asked that."

Lil moved her hands from her face and said, "Sike," and bent over laughing.

"Oh my God, that was so mean, Aunt," Ayana said, clutching her chest. "I thought you were for real crying."

"Will that teach you not to ask inappropriate questions?"

"Prolly not."

"Well, good, because for real, for real, as you all say, you can legit ask me anything. And I didn't have children because, honestly, I didn't want to. I didn't really want to get married, didn't want to have to go through the whole baby-daddy thing. I was kinda married to my work. But basically, I simply did not want to have children. And I'm totally okay with that."

"That's more than I got from Aunt Bev, though admittedly I

was maybe nine when I asked her, and she said she chewed too much ice when she was little and it froze her ovaries."

"Aunt Bev ought to be 'shamed of herself telling such tales," Lil said, rolling her eyes.

"I actually believed her till I was about fourteen and realized no way that's true."

"So why the preoccupation with having babies?" Lil asked, looking at Ayana's stomach when she did.

"Yo, I am so not pregnant," Ayana said. "Please, I've disappointed my parents enough for one lifetime."

"No, you haven't. You're twenty-two, trust me, you're apt to disappoint them a few more times, at least."

"My mom for sure."

"I surely disappointed my mother."

"And GG?"

"Oh God, definitely GG," Lil said.

Ayana had been moving the swivel chair in semicircles, one leg curled under her, her other foot swiping the luxury vinyl plank floor rendered as zebrawood. She pointed her toe to stop the chair so that she and Lil were face-to-face. Finally, the chance to satisfy the question that had plagued her for years: What happened between her and GG that was so egregious that her name could not even be whispered in GG's presence? But in the second it took for Ayana to still the chair, it was already too late. Lil was already seeing that day. She was dressed for *The Mike Douglas Show* in her navy suit and crisp sky-blue shirt, her fuchsia, purple, and white handkerchief fanning out from the suit's breast pocket. GG was on the porch as Lil prepared to leave the house. Lil was so nervous, GG so calm. She looked up from the burgundy leather Bible on her lap, she put her magnifying glass on the table and closed the Bible and tilted her cheek for Lil to kiss her forehead goodbye, the way she always kissed her before she left the house. When Lil stood from her lean, GG stood, too. "What's your appointed time?"

"My appointed time?" Lil asked, as she repositioned the strap of her shoulder bag higher on her arm, pushing it against the handkerchief. "I mean my start time is what it always is."

"You're leaving earlier than usual," GG said. She reached up to adjust the handkerchief, then pulled it from the pocket completely, then told Lil to hold out her hands. Lil did, wondering if her grandmother wanted to see if her hands were shaking. She managed to keep them steady as GG spread the handkerchief over them, then folded the square into a diamond, and folded it again, and again, and gently pushed it back into Lil's breast pocket. Lil could feel GG's fingers against her heart, insistent, but also soothing as she arranged the handkerchief. "Ah, look what I just did. A perfect three-point pocket square," GG gushed. "Your grandfather taught me how to do that." Lil had never seen her grandmother revel in her own accomplishments as she did in that moment. It crushed her even now to think about it, given what happened just a few hours later. Even the air around the couch where she sat now winced in pain as the memory moved through her.

Ayana could see the jags the air made. She knew instinctively she couldn't ask Lil such a thing. Not yet. So she continued talking about herself. She told Lil that she knew her mother would go apoplectic, but she was thinking about moving.

"To where?" Lil asked, sitting up again, recovered.

"Well, I was thinking about asking GG and Aunt Bev if I could move in with them."

"And you think it'll be easier living there?"

"Not easier, but definitely more fulfilling. They could use my help. I mean it's basically GG and Aunt Bev, and Grandmom, when she's up to it. And stuff is getting weird over there. I popped over between shifts at the café, and this little fart of a white man rings the bell and says he has a cease-and-desist order related to some BS about a law against fortune tellers. And GG told him to get off her property, she was not some snake-oil-selling fortune teller. And he said he had a complaint, and she had to appear in court because there was a law against fortune telling in the Commonwealth of Pennsylvania. And he left the summons.

"And then last week somebody from Licenses and Inspections was there and said there was a complaint about the structural integrity of the house."

"The structural integrity?"

"Weird, right? It's feeling orchestrated to me."

"I gotta say, I'm not liking the sound."

"And last week GG met with a seeker, and I took notes. He was describing his concern over certain developers deflating property values using a variety of tactics so that they can buy the dip with the real estate. And I know someone who works in affordable housing who said that the area will no longer be affordable in a minute."

"Your green-eyed friend?"

"I mean, casual friend, yeah, but him."

"Nice young man. What's he do, exactly?"

"He's like an advocate, but he's frustrated 'cause he said there're too many people with divided loyalties, especially in upper management, working more for developers than the neighborhoods."

"I'mma talk to your aunt Bev in the morning, and you should get some rest."

"Okay, but you don't think anybody would bomb the house, do you?"

"Bomb the house, no. What's got you thinking such a such thing?"

"Hate is real," Ayana said. Then she kissed Lil good night and went to bed reluctantly. She wanted to talk. Wanted to tell Lil more about the seeker who she'd thought was signaling to them to watch their backs.

18.

Fortune Tellers

Lil had back-to-back doctors' appointments the next day. Met with the general oncologist, who put such a rosy picture on her condition that she told herself, "You got this, girl." Then she met with the surgeon who'd do the liver resection if she chose that route. Came back down to earth when she learned the recovery time could be at least a couple of months. Then got more sobering news from the GI doc, who ticked off statistics about how many people survive a month, two months, six months after the procedure. The interventional radiologist who would ablate the tumor provided a more hopeful view, except that the lesion was very close to the diaphragm, so it would prove difficult to ablate. The general radiologist was confident, though, that they could target the proton right at the lesion.

After all of that, she learned that she was hypoglycemic and prescribed a glucose monitor and given an instruction sheet on foods to avoid, strategies for timing her meals, symptoms to look out for. She considered this newest malady small potatoes next to liver cancer. Folded it all away in her purse and the back of her mind.

She wished she'd brought someone with her who could take notes and ask questions she didn't know to ask. Lorna had offered to come, but Lil wasn't ready to disclose her diagnosis. She would before she started treatment, but she had a couple of weeks, at least, until then. She wanted to forestall for as long as possible the looks she'd get from Miles and Lorna, their eyes welling up as if she were already dead. As it was, that was why Bev hadn't told her about the license and inspections person showing up there. Or the person with the summons accusing them of being fortune tellers. "Fortune tellers, really, Bev. And you didn't call me," Lil yelled into the phone.

"Look, the whole thing is so absurd, I thought it was a prank. And you need to stay focused and calm to prepare for your treatment. You don't need dumbass distractions. GG's got a good lawyer in that back pocket of hers where she stores all the services we need and then some. It's already handled."

"I hope, because a law against fortune telling is a thing in Pennsylvania."

"And what fortune tellers live here?"

"We know that, Bev, but some shady complainant could make a case, and the family could get dragged into court, and with social media, what happens here is around the world in a nanosecond."

"Look, baby sis, you're still post-traumatic from what that

Mike Douglas and crew did to you decades ago. GG's not worried, so neither am I."

Lil asked Bev then what she'd wanted to ask the moment she touched down in Philadelphia but hadn't because part of her didn't really want to know. "Does GG know I'm back?"

"She does."

"You told her?"

"I did."

"Did you tell her why?"

"Absolutely not."

"Well, how did she react, you know, just to the news that I'm back in Philly?"

"Girl, Mama cried like a baby."

"I didn't ask how Mama reacted, I asked how GG reacted."

"About how'd you expect for a tough-as-nails old broad who still knows everything."

"You're not answering me, Bev. What? Did she say I was dead to her, or I better not step foot in that house, or what?"

Bev's voice turned down, and Lil guessed her face did, too, because it saddened Bev, too. "She didn't say anything. She didn't react at all."

Lil was sitting in the hospital pavilion where the glass ceilings showed the sky that was blue with an occasional fleck of pink, a white pom-pom here and there floating by. A lone blue balloon sailed up and up, likely broken free from the bunch that was to be someone's leaving-the-hospital present; she watched it soar with intention, heaven bound.

19.

Freedom

Lil was curled up in her favorite spot, the butter-soft couch in the family room that would serve as the cover art for Lorna's home design website. She was playing Spelling Bee and had just reached the rank Amazing and was trying to get to Genius when she heard the window in the unfinished part of the basement creak open. She knew it was Ayana. She'd been aware of Ayana's propensity to come and go through the basement window like that when she was getting in especially late. The first time it happened, Lil pretended to be asleep on the couch down here so Ayana could tiptoe on past her and get upstairs. She didn't want her presence in the house to be a disruption to them, especially not to Ayana. She knew how treacherous the early twenties could be. She listened to Ayana jump down to the floor.

Lil loved that child. She wanted to help her navigate the land mines of being a young Mace woman, the oppositional pulls of obligation to family versus obligation to herself. Freedom and the complicated shape it would take in her life.

She put her phone down and snuggled under the cashmere throw and closed her eyes, all ready to feign sleep until Ayana walked through to get upstairs, or until she herself fell asleep for real. So easy to fall asleep here because of the way the couch seemed to fold itself around her, the way the cashmere touched her gently, the relax-yourself glow of the lamplight, the settling-in feel of being back in Philadelphia in her brother's house, the way reconnecting with Lynn and Charise warmed her heart, and the way being so close to Bev again, seeing her in the flesh and not over FaceTime, was beginning to repair it.

She felt herself drifting into a sleep that was soft as velvet. She hoped death would feel this good.

Ayana could see the glow of the light coming from the better part of the basement. She knew Lil must be on the couch, so she rested on the stool until she was sure her aunt was asleep. She loved having Lil with them. Loved her energy and her easy manner. Loved how engaged with life she was. Even though Lil had been away from Philadelphia for decades, she'd reconnected with her friends and was always out somewhere. Sometimes Ayana could hear her sitting on the steps out in the backyard, just under Ayana's bedroom, giggling on her phone like a teenager. Her laughter was like music.

Ayana especially appreciated the way that Lil's presence reordered their lives so they were putting their better selves on display—her parents were arguing less and even sharing the same bedroom again to keep up appearances for Lil. And Ayana was being that good daughter, working earnestly at the café, helping around the house without being asked, holding her tongue when she wanted to argue with her mother, which was often, and trying instead to understand her mother's point of view, which she rarely succeeded at.

She still fell short when it came to the late nights, though, and fell even shorter when it came to juggling two men. She considered her need to be with both Moe and Cue her largest failing, because no one else knew. And the things no one else knew pierced the most.

Especially of late, because after Cue appeared in the café, and she'd gone home with him and spent the afternoon, it was the first time they'd been together when the catalyst for their being together had not been Ayana needing relief from the aftermath of a Knowing. She could no longer use the justification that he kept her from spiraling toward a mania that she feared she'd not recover from. Not after they'd ended up at his Lincoln Drive apartment that afternoon. And again a few nights later. And again tonight. She was still tingling from their time tonight, and this was supposed to be her night with Moe. But Moe had texted her earlier to cancel, a fraternity thing that he couldn't get out of. She was relieved, although she had just picked up another whopper-size Tootsie Pop for him. She'd actually thought about offering it to Cue, then chided herself for the thought, even as she pondered what it meant that she'd even had the thought.

She pulled the lollipop out now and unwrapped it as quietly as she could so her aunt wouldn't hear her. She rolled the lollipop around in her mouth. It was sweet, like her thoughts of Cue rolling around were sweet. She liked that he never brought up the things she told him when she was in that fraying, unraveling state. Never questioned her about the results of what she'd seen—had it come true? Even after he'd met Lil at the café that morning, he didn't ask, *Is she the one you saw fall when you saw the house fall?* Just said, "Your aunt's a seriously cool lady."

"I can't agree with you more," Ayana said, wondering all over again what Lil could have done to make GG send her away.

Ayana gnawed on the high part of the lollipop stick as she thought back to the time when she was a child and heard Lil's name mentioned in her great-grandmother's presence. That was the same day she realized she could never admit to GG that she'd been experiencing Knowings, too.

Ayana had been ten years old, and GG had just presented her with an elaborate dress of velvet and lace and silk trimmed in organza. She told Ayana it was her first ritual dress because that very morning she would participate in a ritual. Ayana was sky-high-excited as she squealed and jumped up and down and ran to her great-grandmother and hugged her.

GG told her to settle down because she first had to tell her a story. She told Ayana the story of Luda without saying Luda's name, called her their Mother Ancestor, the name they used around the younger Maces who'd not yet taken their vows.

Ayana was mesmerized by a young girl so freely able to express what she'd seen, to be so adamant about it with Ragman Blue that he believed her and became to her Mr. Blue. She had the thought, as she listened to GG, that if she had been more adamant with her mother, insisted she knew the car was going to crash through the Marshalls window before it did, that maybe her mother would have believed her, too.

She stepped into the dress with GG's help. She felt like a princess as she fingered the variations in the soft places from the velvet to the silk to lace. She felt pure. She sat back down on the ottoman that faced GG's recliner. She wanted to tell her great-grandmother the truth about herself, that she, too, had inherited the Knowing gene. But she didn't want to hurt her mother, even as she wondered why being honest with GG would hurt her mother. She cleared her throat, which was suddenly dry, scratched. She could feel her great-grandmother's eyes on her, as if GG knew exactly what Ayana needed to say but didn't know how. GG's expression nudged her on, telling her that whatever it was, she could let GG in.

But right then the bedroom door pushed open, startling them both.

"Who's busting into my room like a hyena?" GG said.

Bev stepped into the room. "I'm sorry, GG," Bev said. "But Aunt Helene is insisting—"

Then Helene barreled in behind Bev. "What's this I hear about this little one taking part in rituals?" Helene motioned to Ayana.

"I don't know what you heard, Helene," GG said.

"Yeah, you do. And it's obviously accurate, because you already got her dressed."

"And your point, Helene?"

"You know she's too young. You know you're showing favoritism. You're making my great-grands wait until they're twelve."

"She's smart for her age," GG said.

"And the ones who have to wait till twelve are stupid?"

"Look, they're all smart. But I see what I see. I know what I know. Okay?"

"Not okay, GG." Helene pumped her fists in the air to the rhythm of her words. "You claimed to see something in Lil, and what did she do? Make a mockery out of the family's gifts for her own enrichment."

Ayana's head volleyed back and forth between Helene and GG. She was looking at GG when Helene said the part about Lil. She watched her great-grandmother turn to stone, not a smooth stone like marble, or the pink stones their ancestor set out to find that morning; she appeared like a massive stone that had just been hammered, now cracked, threatening to crumble. Ayana was terrified.

GG moved the heating pad she had wrapped around her hip and stood slowly. "You know that name is not to be spoken in this house."

"Well, I just spoke it, because you need a periodical reminder that you are not always right."

Bev rushed to where GG stood. "It's okay, GG, you don't have to engage, please don't." Then she turned toward Helene.

"With all due respect, Aunt Helene, you need to get out of my grandmother's room."

"I suggest you remember your place, niece," Helene said. "This is between sisters; you of all people should understand that, the way you been sneaking off all these years to go see that turncoat sister of yours."

The door pushed open again; this time it was Carlotta. "You better not be in here disrespecting my grandmother," Carlotta said as she moved right toward Bev. Bev stood in front of her, shoulders squared.

Ayana knew that Bev and Carlotta had a huge dislike for each other. She also knew that Bev was a fighter. One of the younger cousins' favorite stories, which they would tell when they played together after a ritual feast, was of Bev taking down the man who'd gotten in GG's face.

As Ayana watched Bev's shoulders unfurl like those of a boxer warming up, she felt her own body trembling the way it had when she knew beforehand that the red MINI Cooper would explode through the Marshalls window. She saw Bev grab Carlotta by the shoulders and shake her. She saw GG moving toward them, trying to get between them, to separate them, telling Bev that this was not her battle, "not yours, either, Carlotta." Then Bev pushed Carlotta away from her, pushed her so hard that Carlotta fell into Helene, knocking her down. Ayana heard the trumpet of footsteps blaring up the stairs, and her whole family crowded into GG's bedroom: GG and Helene's middle sister, Flora, her grandmother Hortense, the great-aunts' daughters and granddaughters, even the re-

Family Spirit

sentments accreted through the years crowded in, the rivalrous envy over GG's elevated status as the oldest, the decision-maker, the money counter, crowded in too; they shoved and knocked into each other, slapping and punching and flailing, screaming and cursing. And then the men—her father, Miles, among them—the men who sidelined themselves during ritual time crowded in, too. They tried to unscramble the massive wreck of bodies to get to the bottom of the pile, to see who was under the pack, that one most likely severely hurt. And when they did, people hollered, "Mercy, no, Lord, please, please. No!"

Ayana's eyes were squeezed shut. When she opened them, she saw only GG and Bev and Helene in the room. Had it been a Knowing, or was it what her dad always joked was her over-active imagination when she was younger and she'd scene out playdates with her make-pretend friends. She wasn't sure and couldn't chance that it was just her imagination as she ran to Bev and grabbed her around the waist and burrowed her head in her stomach, moaning, "No, Aunt Bev, please don't hurt Aunt Helene, please don't."

She felt Bev's arms around her, heard her voice saying, "It's okay, Yanna, we're okay, you're okay."

Ayana watched GG sit back down and take in deep breaths of air. She watched the rise and fall of GG's chest calm to a slower, steadier rhythm. She saw Helene's tightly fisted hands loosen into fingers gently curled. She felt the ire ebbing that had erupted when she heard the utterance of Lil's name.

From childhood until now, Ayana never learned what exactly her aunt Lil had done to make GG react so to the sound of her name. She just knew that her great-grandmother's wrath at hearing Lil's name, and her own inability to confess to GG that she, too, could see into the future, were forever linked.

Now she was back to where she always landed when she mourned her inability to share her foretelling ability with her family. She was back to resenting her mother for forcing her to deny who she was.

Her teeth tore into the top of the lollipop stick as she sucked on it furiously. She could see her mother's face so clearly, her cheekbones hardened, her eyes watering as she begged Ayana not to be like those Maces, as if Ayana could help it, as if she were saying, *Don't wear the gray dress, wear the brown one.* And Ayana tried, she really did try, to deny her alikeness to her father's family, to her family. And now she'd had the vision that the Mace family home would explode. And she couldn't say anything to anyone, just Cue, who likely didn't even know what the hell she was talking about.

Damn, Mom, she screamed in her head. Why'd you have to be so, so you? Why couldn't you let me be me? What am I supposed to do now?

Fuck. Now she was doing what she always did when she felt this level of resentment toward her mother. To try and rid herself of the guilt, she swallowed it. Swallowed it all, the resentment, the anger, the fear. And then she swallowed the lollipop, too. The mammoth ball that was the perfect fit for her throat separated from the stick after her biting and tugging it in frustration. Her throat cradled the sugary ball as if it were a swaddled newborn. She gagged and tried to force it up. She thought that she would be okay if she could just let air out, because then new air would rush in. "Nature abhors a vacuum," her high school science teacher had drilled into them, because they needed to understand it as a scientific fact but also as a fact of life. "Choose wisely the things that will rush in to fill your empty places," she'd caution, and Ayana sensed she was talking only to her.

She pondered if nature abhorring a vacuum was as true in death as it was in life. Surely she was dying as she tried to will the ball to move up or down so she could breathe. But only the darkness was moved. It was both soft and hard as it covered her, rendering her emptier than she'd ever been, and then rushing in to fill her up.

Up and up, as she felt her chest being lifted up, her rib cage lifted up so high. She had KC and the Sunshine Band in her head, singing about getting lifted high, high, high. Her father loved that song. Would she miss him when she was gone, or was the missing one-sided because the people left behind didn't know what the dead knew? The power of her lifted-up ribs forced the cherry ball to shoot from her mouth, and she could gasp. She could breathe. She could cry. She could hold on to Aunt Lil, who was turning her around, calling her name. "Yanna, Yanna. Yanna," she repeated.

She fell into her aunt's arms, she coughed and sobbed and spat and, finally, she could speak. "Aunt Lil," she said between breaths, "you're gonna die." And then she clung to her aunt and just cried.

Lil settled Ayana down and covered her with the cashmere throw and went to make her chamomile tea, heavy on the honey. As she was pouring water over the tea, Lorna sauntered into the kitchen as if she were on a fashion runway in her matching light blue silk set—pajamas, robe, bonnet. "I thought I heard shouting, everything okay?"

"Girl, I'm trying to teach Yanna how to play pinochle," Lil said as she watched relief cover Lorna's face, softening it. "Then Miss Thing has the nerve to beat me the first game."

"She's a quick learner," Lorna said. "I just wish she'd apply her smarts to getting a darn degree."

"Degrees come in all forms. She'll get what she needs. We all do," Lil said as she stirred the honey briskly and watched Lorna yield the tiniest nod. Lil knew that was a huge concession for Lorna, who'd generally push back against any notion that it was okay for her daughter not to finish school; that would be worse than wearing out-of-style skinny jeans. Lil returned the nod and went back downstairs. Apologized in her head to Lorna about Lorna equating a college degree with fashion sense. She knew Lorna wasn't that superficial, even if Bev thought so.

She handed Ayana the tea and sat in the swivel chair. Ayana's breaths were catching sharply after crying so hard. The space around them was otherwise silent. Lil had respect for silence, its contradictory ability to be soft without relinquishing itself, to be still even as it was filled with movement, amorphous and also focused. So focused. She focused on the realization moving softly, twirling through the stillness as she allowed the awareness to settle.

Family Spirit

"You had a Knowing about my death?" she whispered.

Ayana nodded as she sipped the tea. The honey coated her throat and felt like heaven.

"You've had Knowings always?"

"Yes," Ayana said emphatically. Said it with her whole self. This felt like heaven, too. To admit such a thing to someone who knew that thing intimately.

"And of course you couldn't tell GG, or your grandmom, or your aunt Bev, because it would devastate your momma."

Ayana nodded. She was crying again. This time relief tears, the best kind, better than tears of joy because even joy meant having to reassemble things to accommodate it, like having company you love come for dinner, you've still got to prepare the house, got to cook, do dishes after; even joy could be work. But these tears were wonderfully new for her. These tears weren't bringing, they were deleting. She felt the deletion draining the years of guilt for lies she'd told to hide herself.

Lil allowed the silence to glimmer as Ayana sipped her tea. "So the cancer will kill me," she said as a matter of fact.

Ayana sat all the way up, her eyes bulging. "You have cancer?" she said in a loud voice.

Lil motioned for her to take her voice down. "Didn't you say I was going to die, you had a Knowing? Isn't that what you said?"

"But not from cancer," Ayana tried to whisper, but her louder voice kept breaking through. "No, not cancer. Where is it, is it in your breast, please don't tell me it's triple negative."

"Well, wait. First tell me what you saw."

"I saw the house explode."

"The house explode? Which house? Not the Mace house?" Now it was Lil's turn to raise her voice.

"Yes, exactly that house."

"Oh my God," Lil said, feeling stricken. "I saw the same thing years ago. Right before I left Philadelphia. I thought it was a metaphor for other things."

Ayana pulled the throw from around her so she could also talk with her hands, her shoulders, as she mimicked an explosion. She described Luda's rainbow falling from the ceiling, described the beam falling, even described the beam hitting Lil, knocking Lil to the floor. "Did you see all of that?" she asked. "Did you see yourself falling?"

"Just the house. That's all I saw. Just the house."

Ayana felt herself shaking as she watched her aunt's rankled reaction. She thought she was beginning to descend into that horror of post-Knowing madness. Thought she needed to leave here, needed to get to Cue so he could circumvent it, so he could calm her. Her phone was in the back part of the basement, and she stood to go get it, but then she sat back down. Lil was next to her, her arms around her, rocking her.

Lil began to sing the song they always sang during the rituals she'd grown up with, when one of them came to know something that brought them to their knees. She'd not uttered that song in decades, and the words flowed from her lips as if she'd been singing it every hour of every day.

Pour back into us your peace that we let go, the gift,
the glorious gift,

Family Spirit

calm us with your glow, from head to heart to soul,
  to make us whole,
that we may know. The gift, the glorious gift.
Oh, sweet, sweet Spirit, calm us with your glow,
that we may know. That we may know.

She sang it again, and again, and again. She could feel Ayana settling down, could feel herself settling, too. And now Ayana was singing. Such a sweet sound to hear her niece sing the same song Lil had grown up with. She saw herself then, dancing under Luda's rainbow with her family, the air stretching to accommodate them all as one, and in those precious moments they were one, connected, regarding, communing, loving. She pulled Ayana up, and they began to dance like swans, arms going high and low, twirling. They held hands and spun each other around. Expanding and releasing, taking in what they needed, letting go of what they did not.

And then Lil whispered the name of Luda, and Ayana whispered it back to her. Back and forth, the call-and-response making the smallest ripples in the air. Lil had not put breath to that name since she'd said it to Kevin that night. She'd not heard the sound of that name touch her ear since the last ritual under her grandmother's watch. She felt her chest widen, felt her whole self lighten. Free. That was it, she realized. She'd traveled the world; advised CEOs, the uber-wealthy, the connected, even once a king, about what the future might hold; in the process, she'd amassed the means to go where she wanted, when, and how. But it was here, in her hometown in the basement of her baby brother's charming house, dancing with her niece, as they breathed the name Luda, it was in this moment that she was free.

Ayana found a newness in this moment, too, as she danced with her eyes closed, unaware of the blue silken cloud watching her from the top of the stairs, and then she was aware as the cloud moved slowly down. Such a light touch Lorna had always had, a bounce to her gait, head high, shoulders low and squared. She'd tried to teach Ayana to walk like that, even paid for charm school, but walking like a model was never on Ayana's list of aspirations. Though she felt like one now as she floated toward her mother, who looked at her with soupy eyes the way she'd looked at her after the car went through Marshalls. "Ayana, what am I seeing?" Lorna asked.

"Me, Mom, please look closely, 'cause you're seeing me, you know, the total me. Mom, I always could see things. Always. See me. Please, Mom, please, please, see me."

Lorna sat on the steps, her shoulders slumped like they rarely did, slumped the way they did when she tried to convince Ayana that there was no way she'd been able to know the red MINI Cooper would crash through the Marshalls window before it happened. Impossible, she'd insisted. Simply impossible.

Ayana squeezed in on the step next to her mother. She took Lorna's hand in her own. Lorna squeezed Ayana's hand. She did at least do that.

The End?

January 2020, Nona's Writing Room, Philadelphia Exurbs

Nona was exhausted inside and out. She'd just finished packing away Christmas decorations in the exurban house that was larger than necessary for two people, and unforgivable in size for just one, which might be the result now that her world had blown up. After she and Bob left the church where the cutest child was hilarious as he pantomimed "Little Drummer Boy," Bob admitted to fathering a son with a flight attendant on a layover. A layover! A married pilot fucking a flight attendant on a layover. How clichéd, how unimaginative and unoriginal and stale, she'd raged at him, piling on the redundancies as she characterized his infraction as if the worse part of what he'd done was the banality of it all, the colorlessness.

He begged her forgiveness. He still loved her, only her, he swore. His remorse leaked from his pores and settled at their feet like an oil slick. She had to hold on to him until she could get beyond the slipping and sliding to where she was now. Where she always found her traction. At her desk.

She opened her laptop. She hit the find function, then entered the page number; she knew the exact page number that began the scene in the café when Ayana was shocked by Cue's presence and astonished even more when Lil sauntered in. Nona surprised her own self as she'd constructed that scene.

She had intended to zero in on the story Miss Dot would tell Moe. Miss Dot was animated, funny, and her voice would bring a bit of comic relief. But as Nona described the corner where Moe and Miss Dot sat, the coated windows, the two-person rounded table, Miss Dot's *Philadelphia Tribune* peeking from the top of the vinyl shopping bag hanging from her chair, she noticed the off-kilter vibe of things. Miss Dot was unusually tense, her arms folded close into her chest. She periodically rocked back and forth as if soothing a crying baby. Moe's jawline was hardened, his eyes not leaving Miss Dot's face as he reached out to squeeze her arm, consoling her. Nona was frightened. She pulled back. She redirected the scene to Cue, to Lil. Such sweet thickness their surprise appearances made, like cake batter. Nona would have to stir around for days to blend the ingredients and smooth them out. She welcomed the distraction from the story Miss Dot yearned to tell, that Nona didn't want to hear.

She was tired of fighting now. She returned to that café scene armorless. No breastplates, no shields. She allowed Miss Dot her say.

"Yeah, baby, right at the Aqua Lounge," Miss Dot said to Moe, as he leaned his head closer in because her voice was uncharacteristically quiet.

"I was at the Aqua Lounge that day. I remember 'cause their special was fried butter fish and candied yams. The place was packed with people coming in to buy a platter. I had just picked up my tin of Anacin from the Sun Ray and that butter fish

Family Spirit

smelled so good, it was like the aroma seeping out was curling its fingers, motioning for me. First thing I saw once I got inside and my eyes adjusted to the blue lights was that girl in the middle of the dance floor doing that bop. Lord that girl could dance. All she wanted to do was dance. She'd dance in clubs, she'd dance on the street, she'd go to house parties where she wasn't even invited and kick up her heels and take over the dance floor, and they tell me people would make a circle around her and clap and cheer her on and she was so good they'd take up a collection and she'd leave those parties with a nice amount of walking 'round money. The problem though was that her wanting to dance all the time didn't fit in with the rest of her life. She had a cute little daughter, a handsome husband, a nice little house on Ithan Street with a settling-in porch. But they say her husband didn't want her to dance. Her mother, either. They both demanded she stop with all the dancing and concentrate on keeping house like she belonged to do. And I do believe she tried to stop. But if a thing is in you, and you tell yourself it's not, it's just gonna grow, it's just gonna get bigger and meaner, then it's gonna burst on out of you like a monster, a monster that you created 'cause you tried to keep the doggone thing locked up inside you in the first place. So, when she tried but couldn't stop, her husband took the little girl from her. But he wasn't equipped to raise her by himself, so he took the child to his mother-in-law, said 'I need your help, I need you to take over with this here grandchild of yours, cause your daughter can't do right by her.' The grandmother refused. Said she'd be doing the devil's bidding by making it easier for her daughter to stay out in the streets dancing. Imagine that. I guess the grandmother didn't know any better. And the boy started crying, asking her what was he supposed to do. So the grandmother suggested his sister, who was already raising three girls of her own, and by all accounts doing a superb job. At least the grandmother was right about that. They say her aunt took the little girl in and raised her with the same love she had for her other three. Gave her a good upbringing, dance classes, piano lessons, girl scouts, even had her singing in the children's choir at that highbrow Baptist church. Yeah, thank God at least she did fine. But poor Francis, that was the dancer's name, I do believe she wouldda made the big time 'cause the promoters and the talent people was all up and down Fifty-Second Street checking out the acts. Only a matter of time before she was discovered and put on the big stage dancing in a musical. But the poor little thing took sick. Started losing weight; they say she would dance a spell, then have to find somewhere to sit. Got thin as a toothpick. Clothes started hanging off of her. But she still danced. Lord, did she still dance. She left this earth dancing. I was a witness sitting up there waiting for my platter, hoping they wouldn't run out of candied yams as they were known to do. She was doing that bop like nobody's business, her shoulders in it, stepping to the beat, and adding her own steps and still keeping time with her partner as he twirled and twirled her. I don't know if she got dizzy or if she lost her footing. But she went down on the dance floor that day at the Aqua Lounge. And she never got up. They say she had a cancer that had spread all through her body."

Miss Dot shook her head back and forth as if she still couldn't believe it. She looked away from Moe and rubbed her hands up and down her arms.

"You chilly, Miss Dot?" he asked. "You want my jacket?"

"No baby, just makes me shudder sometimes, how I judged that chile like she was a devil. And I have and still do ask the good Lord to forgive me 'cause she just wanted to dance. She just needed permission. I wish I wouldda found it in my heart to give her permission." She sat straight up then. "I mean, not me, of course; I had no say over her. I wish her mother, her mother, her mother is what I meant to say." Moe was already squeezing her arm, even as she tried to correct herself, saying how sorry he was for her, for everyone.

"Miss Dot," Moe whispered, "her mother did the best she could. And I'm sure if Francis was here, she'd be the most forgiving person. I'm sure of that."

"Thank you, baby," she said, her relief palpable. Her arms untensed, her shoulders lowered, even her voice returned to its usual high volume. "Are you fixing to be late for your class?" she asked, as she grabbed her folded newspaper from her bag. "Am I gonna have to tan your backside with my *Tribune* if you don't hightail it on outta here?"

Moe left, laughing.

Nona liked ending the scene with Moe laughing. Poor Moe. Ayana would have to realize that Moe, whom she adored, was not the man a Mace woman needed. He was a prize for someone with more conventional leanings. All the good women would be fawning over him, Ayana would tell herself to make it easier to let him go.

Nona was still deciding whether or not to let Bob go. Not just because Bob had fathered a son with another woman, even though he swore on the name of his Black—but still too fundamentalist for Nona's likings—Jesus that he didn't love the woman, swore to Nona that he loved only her; but also because he liked wide-open spaces and she liked porches; he liked quiet discussions and she liked loud get-togethers; he liked to plant in neat organized rows and she liked gardens that were lush and wild with chaotic symmetry. He even liked Dallas. But she did love him. She'd just need to forgive him. Like she needed to forgive her grandmother and her father, for not accommodating her mother's dream.

She sighed into quiet air in her writing room. It was time for the what-was-going-to-happen-to-the-Maces to happen. She thought she was finished, though. Thought she should let the Maces write their own ending. They knew best. They always had. Her characters were always smarter than she was: bolder; more insightful; more courageous and adventurous; funnier; more honest, more open; more capable of delighting in discovery. They propped her up even as they provided her a safe place to hide. They instructed; they illuminated paths through the thicket. They were like God in that way.

She'd end her story with one more halibut dinner for Bob when he returned from his latest rotation after a layover that would last who knew how long. They'd talk and cry through it. They'd decide their next forward motion. In the meantime, she'd tell her cousins about the necessity of her MRI. They'd fight over which one of them got to go with her to her appointment. They'd surround her as she visited her mother's grave, where she'd leave the go-go boots she still had packed away in her trunk, the boots so proudly worn by the woman in that bar who'd kissed Lil's cheek, kissed Nona's, too, called her doll, told her she loved her.

She hit save. Tired but now fulfilled, ready for the Maces to bring their story on home.

20.

Silence

Lil and Ayana were up all night. They drank tea with honey, and Lil told Ayana about her cancer, about her life after she left Philadelphia, told her why she'd been banned from the family home, told her about Kevin, *The Mike Douglas Show*, her fall, the explosion she'd thought was a metaphor but now she wasn't so sure. She told her about Lydia, who'd helped her rise. And how much she'd loved putting Ayana's daddy to sleep at night. Told her about her great-grandfather, whom Ayana never knew, who'd remind Lil that when she felt like she was suffocating, the first thing for her to do was breathe. Just breathe.

Ayana listened with rapt attention; she didn't even interrupt Lil with questions, which was unusual for her. Though Ayana did cry when Lil described the peacoat Kevin had left, because it seemed like something Cue would have done, even as she reminded herself that Cue would never be in Kevin's situation because he would never violate trust the way Kevin had. "And, oh yeah," she said to herself, "you're not with Cue anyhow. Moe, remember?" And then she realized, No, not Moe. Moe wasn't built for this. Cue was. Ayana allowed the realization to get in her bones that she'd have to let Moe go. Then she wrapped her arms around Lil when Lil tried to put into words how she'd felt as she stood in front of her home after *The Mike Douglas Show* and held on to Bev, and Bev held on to her, and the words disappeared.

Ayana told Lil about the times she'd have a Knowing and had to keep it to herself, how it made her feel as if she were dying, hyper, and hypersensitive to sounds and sights, and nauseated, and hot and cold, sweats and chills. "It was torture," she said.

"Dear God," Lil said, "I wish I had known. I could have helped you. I would have stood with you in front of GG at dawn, because that's when truths come to her. I would have told her to look at you, to agree that she's never known a more endearing, sincere, selfless, person than you. And she would have. Trust me, Ayana. She knows things, she does, she can see all the way to a person's heart."

"Well, why did she banish you? I think you're all those things, too."

"Because I'm not, Ayana. And GG knew. She could see my dishonesty, my scheming."

"But it wasn't your fault. Kevin's the one who violated your trust."

"But I broke a sacred vow, and I knew what I was doing.

Not consciously, but I knew, I just buried my awareness. That's what I did."

"But, but—" Ayana struggled to come up with more defenses for Lil; she stammered around and settled on "But you're still a good person, Aunt Lil."

"And you're a much better person than I am. I was antsy to get out in the world, and there's nothing wrong with that, should you come to that place. But I was willing to burn the house down to do it. I didn't have the courage to say to GG that I could not replace her, at least not then. I was in my early twenties. Had I said that, we could have negotiated; GG's a master negotiator, and fair. She may have said, *Take five years and we'll see*. And who knows what my life would have been like in five years, but at least I would have spread it all out for her to see. You know, I would have given her the opportunity."

Lil stopped talking. Allowed the silence to snow down again, to cover them. She watched it melt away and leave newness: newness of mind, newness of spirit, newness of intention. Now she watched the blackness push through from the unfinished part of the basement and roll toward her like an ocean wave, wetting her feet with insistent slaps, telling her the stars were brightest now. It was time.

Ayana protested the whole while, listing all the reasons why Lil could not go back in that house. "GG might have a heart attack from the shock of you; Aunt Helene might come after you and all of her great-grandchildren will jump you; there's a ritual this morning, you can't go over there and interrupt a ritual." And finally, she verbalized her true fear. They were in the living room, and Ayana was dressed now in her ritual attire, the sight of her going straight to Lil's heart. "Aunt Lil, when I had the vision of the house exploding, and every time I've seen it since, you're there, you're falling. And I've consoled myself that as long as you don't go in the house, you'll live. Please don't, Aunt Lil, please don't, please don't step inside that house."

Lil had changed into a long purple silk dress with velvet piping. It wasn't an official ritual dress in that it hadn't been made by GG and GG's sisters' hands, but it did have silk; it did have velvet; and now it had her grandfather's handkerchief pinned to the collar. Bev had wrapped it in tissue paper and placed it in the zippered part of the bag she'd packed for Lil that day. Lil had pulled the handkerchief out over the years. She'd rubbed it between her fingers when life got hard, when she'd broken up with the latest man who wanted commitments, conventionality; or when she was dealing with a private client and the situation presented so many complexities and she couldn't see through them into tomorrow; or when she simply missed home. She'd finger the piece of cotton, white-edged with red stitching, and imagine she was talking to him, watching his eyes go soft for her as if she were the best little girl who ever lived.

Lil fingered the handkerchief now. It bolstered her resolve to help Ayana stand before GG with naked honesty the way Lil had not been able to do. "You will tell her simply, clearly, without wavering, that your whole life, the Knowing spirit has inhabited you, and you concealed it, and that has been your failing, and you will do better from here on out. And she will see through to your soul, and she will accept that. We must do this, Ayana. We must," she said, even as she felt shaky inside. She thought her blood sugar might be low as she pictured the handout they'd given her at the hospital. She told herself there would be plenty of food at the after-ritual feast. She reached for Ayana's hand as they walked out the door.

The air was at peak blackness, meaning at any moment the first strands of daylight would be edging through. Ayana said she had no idea where her father's car was parked, and her mother's was in the driveway around back. "But you know my mom never gives up her keys to me, so we should probably take a Lyft." They saw headlights then, saw the car pull up and heard the pop of locks being undone. Saw the interior lights glow and saw Lorna in the car, her face a mass of confusion and acceptance.

"Well, what you waiting for, get in," she said. "I trust you going to GG's, and it looks like you need a ride."

"Oh God, thanks, Mom," Ayana said as she slid into the front seat. "We're trying to beat the clock before sunrise. And you know this is just a drop-off, right, Mom, you know you can't come in."

"Child," Lorna said, and looked over at Ayana, "on what planet, in fact, in what galaxy would I."

The house looked larger. Odd to Lil that it would appear so, because most things she'd encountered from her youth were smaller now: The schoolyard, which had seemed voluminous back when she was sometimes taunted for being a witch, looked the size of a thimble now; the church where the pastor had welcomed them even though the congregation had not—that church now housed high-priced condominiums—appeared minuscule; the corner store where she and Lynn and Charise would meet to buy candy and they'd call her weird because she preferred hot roasted peanuts to a chocolaty, marshmallowy 3 Musketeers bar, and she loved Lynn and Charise even more because that was the thing they found weird about her, that store appeared emaciated, currently home to a vegan bakery that had been at the center of police misconduct when one of Ayana's young friends was tasered by police and left paralyzed just for skipping home, though miraculously, after four years, he was regaining his ability to walk.

The tree out front was larger, too, really much larger, as Lil and Ayana approached the house. The window was open, and they could hear the banter inside as they prepared for the ritual. Such familiar sounds to Lil as she lingered behind the tree, out of view.

"Oh, good, you changed your mind, and you're not coming in," Ayana said, hopeful.

"Indeed I am coming in. But I'll wait until after ritual. Some seeker is anxious for the result, and I don't want to disrupt the process and delay their gift."

"Okay, well, today's is on behalf of the seeker I told you about the other night. The one who was describing the way the developers are buying up whole blocks and using off-book tactics like saying the properties aren't structurally sound to get people to sell for less. He was a bit weird, though."

"How so?" Lil asked as she looked up at the porch with a sense of longing and trepidation.

"Well, I felt like he was saying that part just to get an in, because initially he was saying he was in the midst of a divorce and his daughters were taking sides and it had gotten ugly and he'd been obsessed with a woman he loved years ago and would he ever reunite with the woman from his past. And GG probed, asked about the woman, but then he shut down about the woman he'd been in love with and starting talking about the developers because he was part of a holding company that financed them and he was seeking an answer to should he resign or try to dry up their resources. Afterward, I told GG that his story had holes, and she said she knew, but you know GG, her thing is always, let's see. And knowing GG, she's also likely thinking about bartering to get his intel."

Lil nodded, half listening as she fixated on the porch and on the ground beneath her that felt as if it were shifting. She told Ayana she should get inside. "I'll know by the sounds when ritual time is over."

And then she heard the sounds, heard the first strike of the triangle, then the prayer of purification, not the words, exactly, she couldn't hear the exact words, but she could feel the way the air vibrated. She could follow the crescendos, the pauses, the rush. She didn't need to hear the words; she knew the words, and she matched them to the way the air and the

Family Spirit

tree and the new light above her, the ground beneath her, moved her. And as they began to chant inside and break out in dance, Lil did the same. She heard the babbling then. Knew that the others were surrounding that one as they encouraged her. She heard them saying Bree. Bree. She felt the rush of air even out here. She knew that Bree was relating what she was seeing. She bowed her head in reverence.

She was so woozy that she lost track of time as she stood under the tree with her head bowed. She could tell by the dearth of sounds that they'd moved into the dining room, so she entered the house.

Nobody noticed her because they were tending to Bree, wrapping her in blankets to settle her chills, offering her sips of tea, singing to her their calming song, Ayana hovering over her, adjusting the pillow, asking her what she needed.

The house was exactly as Lil remembered it. Certainly, they had made updates: the new circle rug, the newly painted walls, the newer wing chairs, the wide-slatted blinds. But the air was still the same. Heavy with the weight of obligation and history, and light with the promise of what was to come. That had always been her struggle when she lived here, reconciling the two. Lil took in the assemblage then. Her great-aunts and their daughters were like rare art with their still ravishing eyes, still massive hair, skin smoother than it should be for the years they'd seen. And the younger ones from twelve to Ayana's age were an energetic bounty of potential as they stepped into their calling. "Ah," she whispered into the air as she walked to stand under Luda's rainbow. "Help me to help them, to pour into them what was poured into me. Help me to help them know that though they have individual greatness, abilities, they are also part of something larger than themselves. They are Mace women. That is the source of their power. The family spirit is their power. Oh Lord," she said, no longer whispering. "The family spirit, yes. Thank you, Lord, for the family spirit, Yes, yes, yes." She shouted now.

She felt herself being transported to that place out of reach in ordinary time. This was beyond ordinary. She was entering the place of openness where there was no time, no today, no tomorrow, just space, just blankness, like the blankness Luda saw in the sky that day after the rainbow fell and the vision appeared in the blankness. There it was, for her to see.

Lil began to dance, her eyes closed, her footsteps quickening. It felt as if the gathering in the dining room had migrated to where she was, encircling her. But it could not be, she told herself. Not after her breach, the clean irrevocable cut she'd made from the heart of her family by breaking their most sacred vow. And yet she felt their spirit. Felt that connection to them that was ephemeral, boundless. It would be easier to cut dry air than to sever that, she realized as the spirit of her family passed her from hand to hand, whispered in her ear, encouraging her to let it out, let it go. It was their spirit and their physical selves, too, chanting with her, chanting for her. She felt exalted, loved, even as she felt the room spinning.

She heard GG's voice then. She opened all of herself so that GG's voice would inhabit every fiber of her because it had been so long since she'd heard that voice. "Speak, Daughter of Luda," GG said. And so Lil did.

Family Spirit

She babbled at first about him, about the sweaty ID badge against his chest, his room with no color, that vision she'd had years ago that she'd suppressed. Her unintelligible sounds shaped themselves into words now as she described the explosion, the same explosion she'd seen on the bus that day.

"Where is the explosion?" GG asked.

"It is here," Lil said, crying, shaking.

"What causes it?"

"It is different this time," she said. "This time there are fingers reaching for the switch to explode the house, or is it whole hands, whole systems of inequities, no, this time it is limbs reaching for the switch, pulling the switch to make the house explode."

"Tell me, tell me," GG urged.

"It is a limb no, root. It is the tree root growing under the house. It has taken the easier path and wrapped back around toward the yard, toward the gas main. There it is. The tree root touching the gas main, over and over, chaffing the cast iron gas main. It is exploding. Our house is exploding."

She cried out as she felt the explosion as a whirlwind so powerful, it turned the room upside down. The floor was above her, Luda's rainbow below, the sound of a train running through her head, and then, *boom*. Lil hit the floor hard just like Ayana said that she would.

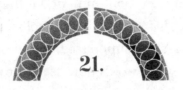

21.

Home?

Lil always thought that if she ever collapsed and lost consciousness as she had at the ritual this morning, that Bev would be the person leaning over her, rubbing her forehead; if not Bev, surely GG, if not GG, certainly Ayana, but here was Hortense. Her lovely mother, her tired mother, her mother whom she'd felt she'd betrayed by working with Lydia. Her mother, still in her ritual garb, was pulling down the railing on the bed in the ER, adjusting the IV dripping liquid into Lil's vein, so that she could practically climb in the bed with Lil. Lil was amazed at her eighty-year-old mother's agility. "Momma," Lil said, as her mother folded herself around her. "Momma, Momma, I've missed you so much, Momma." They snuggled like that until the physician's assistant came in to tell Lil that the seizure—she'd had a seizure after the fall—was caused by severe hypoglycemia.

"You could have died," he said.

Hortense kissed her cheek. "But she didn't," she said. "She didn't."

Thad picked them up from the ER and gave them the news that the gas company confirmed a leak. The main needed replacing. They issued a mandatory evacuation for the entire block in the meantime.

"Evacuation? And go where?" Lil asked.

"I don't know about the rest of them, but your mother and I are checking in at the Embassy Suites in town. Nice little getaway for us. Rumor has that Bev and GG will pile in over at Miles and Lorna's."

"You've got to be kidding me," Lil gasped and screamed at the same time. "Oh my God, that's a sitcom that'll write its own script."

"Or a murder thriller." Thad laughed.

"Or both," Hortense said, laughing, too. Lil realized how rare it was for her mother to laugh. She thought her father did, too, because he kept the jokes about the family dynamic rolling until they got back home.

Home? Lil thought about home as Thad helped her out of the car. She walked in the door and Ayana squealed and ran to her. "God, Aunt, I been blowing up Grandmom's phone that she didn't answer so I finally called the ER and they said you'd been discharged."

"I'm good, Booby, just a little blood sugar issue," Lil said. And before she could say more, there she was: GG. Lil was face-to-face with GG after all these years. Though GG wasn't looking at Lil's face. She looked at her belly. She touched the spot where Lil's liver would be. "Right there?" she asked.

Lil nodded.

"You're not dying." GG said. "Do you understand me,

Lillianna? You don't get to die before me." Her voice was stern, her touch against Lil's stomach was gentle. Her eyes were gentle, too, as she moved her eyes to Lil's face. She didn't embrace her with her arms, but she did with her eyes. She held Lil and rocked her, reassured her with her eyes.

That day they had a different type of after-ritual feast at Lorna and Miles's. Lorna had gone all the way to Costco and gotten rotisserie chickens, and Bev was so touched by the gesture, she found what she could in Lorna's cabinets and fridge and prepared sides of sweet potatoes and string beans and even made a pan of zucchini bread. Helene and Flora and their offspring, including Carlotta and Bree, and younger cousins whom Lil had only met via Bev's descriptions in their phone calls, and letters, and more recently texts through the years were all there.

They were in that soft time, that congenial, openhearted time, as Lil continued to think about home. The house next door to Lorna and Miles was for sale. A double lot with possibilities for expansions. More than enough room for rituals, after-feasts, grandnieces and -nephews and cousins. Even space for Lorna to set up her design studio.

She became so enamored of the idea that two days later, she didn't even cry when they received word that the Mace house had exploded. The gas company had left for the day, but defiant tree roots had accomplished what they'd been working toward for decades. The massive oak tree planted by GG's father tumbled on its side. It's lush head of hair created a nice landing spot for Luda's rainbow to rest intact, nary a scratch on its prized stained glass.

Family Spirit

And then this happened: A note arrived for Lil in a Christmas envelope even though it was July.

> *So sorry about the tragedy. I'm back in Philly, too, if you want to give a shot at being my roommate again. —Kevin*

Acknowledgments

So grateful for my community that surrounded me on this novel's journey: my longtime agent, Suzanne Gluck, whose reading acuity extends beyond the page to even encompass the rooms where a book comes to life; my editor, the gifted Patrik Bass, whose *Knowing* of a story is his superpower; assistant editor Anayaé Holmes, whose efficiency, patience, and support are laudable; James Rahn and the consummate writers and readers of Rittenhouse Writers' Group, whose gems of insight make a story richer; my sisters Paula, Gwen, Elaine, and Vernell, and my niece-sisters Robin and Celeste, who all embody the essence of our parents, grandparents, and ancestors; my children, the two I birthed—Taiwo and Kehinde—and the two I claim—Aaron and Teresa—who help me see what's possible; my grandchildren, Kennedy, Josephine, Ryan, and Michael, who are my joys supreme; and my soulmate, Greg, who makes my world go round.

Family Spirit

And then this happened: A note arrived for Lil in a Christmas envelope even though it was July.

*So sorry about the tragedy. I'm back in Philly, too,
if you want to give a shot at being my roommate
again. —Kevin*

Acknowledgments

So grateful for my community that surrounded me on this novel's journey: my longtime agent, Suzanne Gluck, whose reading acuity extends beyond the page to even encompass the rooms where a book comes to life; my editor, the gifted Patrik Bass, whose *Knowing* of a story is his superpower; assistant editor Anayaé Holmes, whose efficiency, patience, and support are laudable; James Rahn and the consummate writers and readers of Rittenhouse Writers' Group, whose gems of insight make a story richer; my sisters Paula, Gwen, Elaine, and Vernell, and my niece-sisters Robin and Celeste, who all embody the essence of our parents, grandparents, and ancestors; my children, the two I birthed—Taiwo and Kehinde—and the two I claim—Aaron and Teresa—who help me see what's possible; my grandchildren, Kennedy, Josephine, Ryan, and Michael, who are my joys supreme; and my soulmate, Greg, who makes my world go round.

About the Author

Diane McKinney-Whetstone is the author of the critically acclaimed novels *Our Gen, Tumbling, Lazaretto, Tempest Rising, Blues Dancing, Leaving Cecil Street, Trading Dreams at Midnight,* and *Family Spirit*. She is the recipient of numerous awards, including the Black Caucus of the American Library Association's Literary Award for Fiction, which she won twice. A past lecturer at the University of Pennsylvania, her work has appeared in *The Atlantic, Essence, Philadelphia* magazine, and the *Philadelphia Inquirer*. She lives in Philadelphia with her husband, Greg.